JEFF MENAPACE

CALEB
ATONEMENT

Copyright © 2023 by Jeff Menapace
Published by Mind Mess Press
All Rights Reserved

CALEB: ATONEMENT

All rights reserved. Without limiting the rights under copyright above, no part of the publication may be reproduced, stored in or introduced into any retrieval system, or transmitted in any form or by any means (electronic, mechanical, photocopying, recording or otherwise) without the prior written permission of the copyright owner or the publisher of this book.

This book is a work of fiction. Names, characters, places, and incidents are a product of the author's imagination or are used fictitiously. Any resemblance to actual events, locales, or persons, living or dead, is coincidental.

CALEB: ATONEMENT

JEFF MENAPACE

MIND MESS PRESS
2023

might as well have been a starter's pistol: Rosco bolted off towards the nearest tree, where the shit-talking squirrels were stationed, incessant barking matching his lightning speed.

Caleb could not help but smile. Could not help but smile at anything Rosco did, really. His dog's unending quest to catch the squirrels was one of Caleb's favorite sights. Not once had Rosco come close, and not once had he ever been deterred.

Thrill of the hunt, Caleb mused. He could relate. Especially now.

Caleb looked at the man. "So, what brings you here, Misterrr...?"

The man cleared his throat. "Smith. John Smith."

Caleb laughed. "No shit? You're really gonna go with that?"

The man's frown was the flummoxed kind. "I'm sorry?"

Caleb waved a hand at him. "Plenty of time for those in a bit."

"I'm sorry?" the man said again.

Caleb shook his head. "You keep using them all up now and you won't have any left for later. And methinks you're gonna need 'em."

"Need what?"

"Apologies," Caleb said, as though it should have been self-evident.

The man shook away his confusion. "Listen, I don't mean to be rude, but I'm kind of waiting for someone. So, if you don't mind, I'd appreciate—"

"Tommy, right?" Caleb broke in. "Twelve-year-old boy you've been tutoring? Yeah, I spoke to his parents. He's not coming."

The man instantly rose.

"No, no, no..." Caleb said, reaching up and jerking the man back down by the collar with one hand. "Not going anywhere just yet."

"What do you want?" the man asked. His fleshy face, previously red from fight or flight, was now white with dread, betraying his words—it was clear the man knew why Caleb was there.

1

Caleb and Rosco approached the solitary man seated on the park bench.

"Mind if I take a seat?" Caleb asked the man.

The man—flabby, balding, rimless glasses—looked up at Caleb. His jowly face flushed. His pupils dilated. Perhaps he was intimidated by Caleb's size. Or, more than likely, he was intimidated by the fact that Caleb wanted to sit next to *him* when there were plenty of unoccupied benches in the park. Dusk was not far away. The park was empty.

"Actually," the man said, "I'm kind of—"

"'Preciate it," Caleb said, and took a seat next to the man.

Caleb had a backpack with him. He dropped it by his feet, then asked: "Mind if I let my dog off his leash? I know you're not supposed to, but you won't tell, right?" Caleb leaned forward and took hold of Rosco's collar. The beige border terrier whined and wiggled. *Hurry the eff up, Dad,* those whines and wiggles said, *those squirrels over there have been talking all kinds of shit since we got here, and they're not gonna chase themselves.*

When Caleb popped the metal latch free from Rosco's collar, it

Caleb did not answer right away. He instead leaned back and placed both arms lengthwise across the back of the bench, letting out a satisfied groan that coincided with his stretch. He looked east and west throughout the empty park. Rosco could be heard giving the squirrels hell in the distance.

"Park's kinda dead this time of day, isn't it?" Caleb said. "But I suppose you were counting on that, weren't you?"

"Who *are* you?" John Smith asked.

"Well, I could tell ya, but then I'd have to kill ya. Oh, wait..." Caleb looked up at the sky in mock thought, then back down with joyful discovery. He was grinning when he said: "I guess I *can* tell you."

Fear, though keeping John Smith glued to the bench, had not glued the wheels on his cognition; his face showed it.

Caleb laughed again. "I'm *kidding!*" he said, giving John Smith's shoulder a squeeze. "I'm not going to kill you. I made a promise to someone that I wouldn't."

"*Kill* me? Why on earth—promise to *who?*"

Light-switch quick, Caleb's playful manner was gone. "To the parents of the boy you violated."

John Smith's face came alive with hope. "I never touched Tommy! I swear it! I swear it on my mother's soul!"

"And if Tommy had showed?"

John Smith's eyes darted from side to side, the man clearly desperate to come up with something that might grant him a reprieve. He soon did, and he actually looked relieved when he blurted: "But he didn't! He *didn't* show! And thank God...thank God for *you*. I don't know what I might have done if it weren't for you."

"Really?" Caleb said. "Are you really—*fucking actually*—trying to praise your way out of being marked for the pedophiliac piece of shit that you are?"

"*No.* No, no, I was just—"

"Shut up. Just shut the fuck up. This has nothing to do with Tommy."

Flummoxed frown again. "It doesn't?"

"No. I *did* call Tommy's parents, and I *did* tell them not to let him show, but I'm actually here for Justin Ward. That name sound familiar to you by any chance?"

Caleb hadn't even finished "chance?" before John Smith shook his head.

Caleb snorted. "Don't even want to give it a second's thought? Let's try again, and please don't insult me this time; my temper is... unpredictable. Justin Ward—you remember him?"

John Smith looked away. A brief pause and then: "Yes, I remember Justin."

Caleb nodded once—not impressed with the man's honesty, just pleased with it. "Did you know he just had a birthday?"

"No," John Smith replied, still avoiding eye contact.

"Seventeen years old. Though you probably couldn't care less—seventeen's a bit too old for you, isn't it?"

John Smith said nothing.

"Did you know Justin will never see eighteen?"

John Smith brought his full attention back on Caleb.

Caleb fixed his gaze, then slowly mimed sticking a gun into his mouth and pulling the trigger, index finger the barrel, thumb the hammer.

"He...he killed himself?" It was barely a whisper.

"He did," Caleb replied. "Left a note too. I'll give you one guess as to what that note said."

"I wouldn't know."

"I said you could guess."

"I don't want to guess."

"Really? If you're honest with yourself—though I imagine you seldom are—I'd say your odds of guessing correctly are pretty darn good."

"Please don't do this." John Smith looked on the verge of tears.

"Do what, *John*?" Caleb spoke the man's bullshit name with more than a little contempt.

John Smith started to cry.

"Look, I promised I wouldn't kill you, and I meant it," Caleb said. "And I always keep my promises. So, what have you got to lose by being honest with me? They often say there's a special place in hell for people like you. Perhaps owning up to it might make that special place a bit more accommodating." Caleb shrugged and added: "I mean, I'm not really sure how it all works, but you get what I'm saying, yeah?"

Blubbering now. "It doesn't matter if you promise not to kill me. If I go to prison, I *will* be killed."

"Why, John? Why would you be killed in prison?" Caleb's tone was sardonic, his question all but rhetorical.

John Smith just kept on sobbing.

"I'm not going to send you to prison, John. I'd like to; believe me, I would. I'd love nothing more than to have a line of inmates —*big* inmates, if you know what I mean—run an endless train on your ample ass, but one thing keeps me from doing so."

John Smith removed his rimless glasses and wiped away tears. His face was now cautiously optimistic, that of a child who'd been assured he wouldn't be punished despite his inexcusable behavior. "What one thing?"

"Actually, it's a couple of things. Another promise I made, and the fact that I wouldn't be there to see that train in action. Watch you suffer. I'd feel, I don't know, cheated out of something wonderful."

John Smith wiped away the last of his tears and put his glasses back on. The face of the cautiously optimistic child remained. "So, you're not going to kill me, and you're not going to send me to jail…"

"That's right."

"So, what *do* you want?"

"I want you to admit what you did to Justin when he was a child. I want you to admit that you're the reason he took his life on his seventeenth birthday. That *every single fucking day* since your encounter with him years ago was a living hell for the kid. That he felt he couldn't turn to anyone out of such crippling shame for what you'd done. That he felt the only way out was suicide. That's what I want you to admit, John."

Caleb produced Justin Ward's suicide note from his backpack and placed it on John Smith's lap. John Smith looked down at the note but did not touch it.

"Admit it and we're done here, John."

John Smith lifted his head. "We'll be done?"

"Yep."

"I admit it," John Smith said.

Caleb felt a sudden rage. Not for the man's admittance, but for *how* he'd admitted it. There was no shame in John Smith's voice. No regret. His tone was that of a man who was merely saying what wanted to be heard so that he might appease his audience, save his own hide. Caleb fantasized removing John Smith's glasses from his face and jamming one of the frames' temple tips into the sick fucker's eye.

But alas, he could not. His promise.

"Okay—then we're done here," Caleb said.

"I can go?"

Caleb chuckled. "No, no—I said we're done *here*." Caleb casually produced a syringe from his backpack and jammed it into John Smith's thigh.

John Smith managed *"Ow!"* before he was unconscious, his body soon slumping forward and tumbling out onto the grass.

Caleb looked around. The park was still empty, save for a couple walking hand in hand in the distance. Caleb muttered "ah shit" when he saw Rosco approaching the couple, looking for a little love, please.

Caleb stood and bent over John Smith. "Upsy-daisy," he said, hoisting John Smith up and plopping him back onto the bench. It then killed Caleb to do this, but if he didn't want to arouse suspicion when the couple inevitably looked Caleb's way, he would need to put his arm around John Smith and let the man's head rest on Caleb's shoulder, as though they too were a couple, perhaps.

Ultimately, the couple did look in Caleb's direction—they were perhaps fifty yards away—and Caleb waved.

They waved back.

"Sorry about that!" Caleb called to them. "I was just about to put him back on his leash!"

Both the man and woman called back that it was no problem, even commenting on how adorable Rosco was. Caleb smiled and waved to them again. He then called for Rosco.

Rosco left the couple and hurried towards his master without hesitation. The shit-talking squirrels were safe—for now.

When the couple was safely out of sight, Caleb simultaneously pushed John Smith's head away and removed his arm from the man's shoulders. John Smith fell onto his side and lay there like a man napping on a park bench. And why not? He was.

Caleb then fixed the metal latch back onto Rosco's collar, took hold of his leash, and stood. He turned back towards John Smith, checked once more to be sure the park was still empty, then could not resist getting in one good one, driving his fist into John Smith's sleeping face.

John Smith's head shuddered from the blow, but he did not stir.

Caleb then set Rosco's leash on the bench for a moment, told his dog to stay, which he did, then went into his backpack for the third time that day. He pulled out a large canvas sack. Proceeded to stuff John Smith inside, cinching the sack's thick strings tight at its opening.

Satisfied, Caleb put the empty syringe and suicide note back into his backpack and put it on. He then squatted down, took solid hold, and then heaved the canvas bag containing John Smith over one shoulder with little effort.

Taking hold of Rosco's leash again, Caleb started towards his SUV nearby—his dog occupying one arm, an unconscious pedophile the other.

2

Caleb pulled up to the two-story suburban home a few hours later. Night had fallen. Both cars of the home's owners were parked at the curb, just as Caleb had requested—he wanted to use the garage to transport John Smith into their home undetected.

Caleb hit the garage door opener they had given him, waited for the door to rise, and then slowly pulled the SUV inside before hitting the opener again, closing the door behind him.

Before Caleb could even exit his vehicle, the door leading into the house opened. A man and woman—mid-forties—appeared in the doorway. Had grief not done what grief does, they would have been considered an attractive couple. But grief was the undisputed champ when it came to altering one's appearance, and there was no exception here. Both were dead in the face; their posture, impotent.

Caleb killed the engine and exited. He nodded once at the couple.

"Any problems?" the man asked.

"No problems," Caleb replied. "Got everything prepared as we discussed?"

"Yes. Plastic is laid down. Branding irons are in the fire."

"Bags packed? Accommodations taken care of? You're all set to leave right after?" Caleb had told the couple that they would need an alibi as a failsafe should John Smith's disappearance raise questions. As far as friends and family were concerned, the couple had established that, given recent events, they would be going away for a while. Better still, as far as those friends and family knew, the couple had left days ago, their cars on the curb explained with a lie that they would be getting some work done on the house while they were gone; the driveway needed to be available for the contractors, both cars in attendance by the curb because they would be taking an Uber to the airport.

The husband nodded at Caleb. "All taken care of."

"Good. Why don't you two go inside? I'll be in with him in a couple of minutes."

The couple turned and disappeared back into the house. Caleb opened the back door of his SUV, told Rosco to stay, then took hold of the large canvas sack containing John Smith. He was not gentle as he dragged the sack out of the car, letting it drop hard onto the concrete floor like the dead weight it was.

CALEB ENTERED the couple's home, dragging John Smith with him. His backpack from the park was strapped tight to both shoulders.

Duncan and Heather Ward stood silently on the many sheets of plastic covering their den floor. Behind them, the fire in its place thrived. Caleb spotted the branding irons therein, the orange glow of their heads. He felt a tingle of excitement coupled with a tingle of shame. Not an uncommon cocktail of emotions for Caleb. He felt great empathy for the couple, yet the work he so enjoyed was only possible because of their suffering. His work kept him sane. Scratched the itch he wished he'd never acquired. He would take great pleasure in punishing this piece of shit as much as the couple would.

Or perhaps not.

Many of Caleb's clients went through with such jobs out of a need—or duty?—for the justice that had eluded them. Not for the needs that Caleb had acquired. In time, many of Caleb's clients could move on with their lives.

Caleb could not. He was already molded. Turned by the very evil personified by the unconscious man before them now. And this truth produced another polarizing cocktail of emotions in Caleb: anger and delight. Anger for already being turned; delight for cultivating a vocation that allowed him to fulfill needs that some might say were on par with similar desires possessed by evil. But as long as Caleb continued to do what he did, he would never *become* evil (or so he assured himself in private moments that often frightened him), only punish it. Scratch that itch, not with a wicked hand, but a righteous one.

———

CALEB DROPPED the large canvas bag at the feet of Duncan and Heather Ward.

"Is that really him?" Duncan asked.

Although the answer seemed fairly obvious, Caleb was not surprised by the question. In his experience with such jobs, people tended to ask questions with obvious answers. Hearing those obvious answers aloud helped them embrace the real and shed the *sur*real that was all too commonplace with tragedy.

Caleb was happy to oblige. "It is," he said.

Another need to embrace the real: "And he's still alive?"

"He is." Caleb removed his backpack, set it aside, then bent and began working on the canvas bag, soon producing the unconscious, but still-very-much-alive, "John Smith" for them to see, the pedophile's deep snores all the evidence the couple needed.

Caleb tossed the canvas bag into the corner, bent again and checked the plastic zip ties that bound John Smith by the wrist and ankles. He was going nowhere. A large strip of duct tape covered Smith's mouth, amplifying the snores that flapped from his nostrils. He would be saying nothing. Not unless the couple (or perhaps Caleb) wanted to hear him beg.

"Shall we begin?" Caleb started to say, but only got as far as "Shall we—?" before Duncan Ward launched his attack.

A more efficient mode of attack would have been for Duncan Ward to use his shoed feet, the added protection they would provide him, the added damage they would cause. But shoed feet were not intimate. Flesh on flesh was. Intimacy shared love *and* violence; it was all a matter of context.

So Duncan Ward dropped to his knees and began hammering his fist into John Smith's unconscious face, the cracking sound of knuckle on bone waning behind Duncan's increasing, inarticulate cries of rage.

Caleb let it go on for a moment—there would be many methods of catharsis here tonight, and this was one of them.

Turns out, Caleb would not need to interject; exhaustion had stepped in and put a stop to the attack. Or perhaps it was exhaustion and grief, as Duncan Ward was now sobbing uncontrollably, robbing him of any further action. He sat back on his heels, sobbing harder still.

"Okay," Caleb said, bending and taking Duncan beneath both arms and helping him to his feet. "Okay."

Duncan turned and shoved Caleb away before retreating to a corner of the den in a bid to collect himself. Caleb took no offense to this, would have been surprised, in fact, if the man had reacted any other way.

Caleb then turned towards Heather Ward. Her eyes were not on her husband. They were on John Smith, and Caleb recognized what lay behind those eyes all too well.

Round two, he thought.

And round two it was. Only Heather Ward *did* use her shoed feet for her assault, perhaps realizing, after witnessing her husband, that she would inflict more damage by doing so, despite that intimacy of flesh on flesh. And just as Caleb had allowed Duncan Ward to do his thing for a moment, so too did he allow Heather. And while her attack was different, her outbursts were no less heartbreaking than her husband's as she kicked and stomped and cried and screamed and kicked.

Neither exhaustion nor grief seemed to handcuff—or foot cuff, in this case—Heather Ward as they had done her husband; if Caleb didn't interject soon, Heather Ward would kick the man to death, and Caleb did not want that for them. He wanted the pedophiliac prick awake for all that lay ahead, admittedly, shamefully, for himself just as much as for them.

So, Caleb intervened, grabbing Heather Ward around the waist and pulling her off, Heather Ward screaming and sobbing for Caleb to let her go, throwing blind elbows behind her at Caleb's head, kicking at his shins with the heels of her shoes, even throwing her head backwards in an attempt at a reverse headbutt.

And just as it was with Duncan, Caleb took no offense to this either. Again, he would have been surprised if she'd reacted any other way.

Caleb dragged Heather over towards Duncan, who had now collected himself and had been observing his wife's onslaught without any attempt at interference of his own, to which Caleb also understood—she too deserved her turn.

It was only when Caleb managed to lock eyes with Duncan—Caleb's expression asking for help—that Duncan stepped in and took hold of his wife, who then dropped her face into her husband's chest and continued sobbing, Duncan holding her tight, rubbing her back, doing his best to calm her with assurances that all was okay when it was anything but.

Caleb took this opportunity to retrieve his backpack and one of the necessary items therein. Smelling salts.

"Ready to keep going?" he asked the couple.

Duncan and Heather Ward left one another's embrace and faced Caleb. For a moment, Caleb wondered whether they were *not* ready to keep going. Whether what they'd done was enough. Whether Caleb himself could finish the job now and that would be sufficient.

But Caleb was more than a little pleased when he felt the invisible

(*but righteous! Righteous!*)

hand he'd come to know all too well begin to scratch his forever itch when the couple emphatically replied:

"Yes."

3

The heads of the two branding irons sported the same abbreviation: "Pedo."

It had been Caleb's idea. When he'd initially suggested it to the couple, Duncan Ward had produced a curious frown. "But we want him dead," he'd said.

"And?" Caleb had replied.

Heather Ward, immediately cottoning on to what her husband was implying, had added: "What's the point of branding him a pedophile if no one will see it?"

It was a fair point. It hadn't occurred to Caleb that inflicting such excruciating pain onto someone who'd done what this asshole had done needed clarification. Excruciating pain, Caleb felt, was reason enough.

But still, the Wards had a valid argument. They wanted him dead and gone. So why brand the man a pedophile if no one would ever see it?

Caleb had been direct and assuring with his reply. *"You'll* see it," he'd said. "And I'll make sure *he* sees it too. It will also cause him pain unlike anything he's ever felt before in his life ...before we end it. And we will end it." He'd thought about adding: *And it'll be fun*, but had thought better of it. Caleb's eternal struggle that was his constant need for, and enjoyment of, inflicting pain onto those that deserved it shared an awkward room in his psyche with his capacity for empathy.

Empathy and the delight Caleb took in wickedness...Jack Lemmon and Walter Matthau on their worst day could never be such an odd couple.

And so it had been decided. The branding irons would stay. And now it was time.

CALEB APPROACHED JOHN SMITH, who was still unconscious (more so now, and far more "bleedy" than his initial reveal, courtesy of the Wards), but did not use his smelling salts right away. Instead, he pulled a knife from his back pocket and slit John Smith's shirt down the back before removing it.

Duncan and Heather Ward looked on.

Caleb then did John Smith's pants. His underwear too. The man's penis was, to no surprise, flaccid, and rather small to boot. Duncan Ward snorted at this. Caleb could have sworn he'd heard Heather Ward do the same. Good. Still on board; apprehension hadn't crept in, as was sometimes common with clients when things started gathering serious momentum.

Smelling salts still in hand, Caleb started to administer them to John Smith, but was then struck with a lovely idea and immediately pocketed the salts. Instead, he headed towards the fireplace and removed one of the branding irons.

So much better to wake the man with pain.

Caleb decided to do the man's chest first. It seemed as good as place as any. Until a second lovely idea struck him.

Do his ass first. Caleb had to bite down on the inside of his cheek to keep from grinning.

Handle of the branding iron firm in both hands, Caleb pressed the glowing orange head that read "pedo" onto John Smith's right butt cheek. The iron singed the generous flesh, smoke rising from the new mark, the faint smell of singed meat immediate.

And just as Caleb had hoped, the smelling salts would not be needed; John Smith was suddenly very awake, his eyes wider than wide, the muffled scream behind the duct tape louder than loud. Caleb bit down harder on the inside of his cheek and tasted blood; he was close to laughter.

"Morning," Caleb said. "Or should I say, good evening?"

John Smith writhed in agony on the floor. His moans into the duct tape were constant.

"I'd like to introduce Duncan and Heather Ward," Caleb said, gesturing over towards the couple. "Justin Ward's parents."

Despite his pain, John Smith managed to crane his neck towards the couple. His expression was equal parts fear and surprise, and then…shame? Of course shame, Caleb thought. He'd already met the Wards. Several times.

"Oh right," Caleb said. "I suppose an introduction was unnecessary. You've met them before, haven't you? Being Justin's soccer coach for an entire season and all. I imagine your paths had crossed during many a game, yes?" Caleb glanced back at the Wards. "Yes?" he asked them.

Both parents nodded. Duncan Ward said: "We never missed a game."

Caleb glanced back down at John Smith. "Never missed a game. That's devotion, wouldn't you say, John? Especially in today's day and age, what with two working parents being the norm? And you…you had to go and take it all away."

"Why did you call him 'John'?" Heather Ward asked Caleb.

"Believe it or not, he said his name was John Smith. Funny how he stuck with it even after it was pretty fucking obvious what was going on, how and why I'd found him." Caleb nudged John Smith with the toe of his shoe. "Pretty funny, isn't it, John?"

John Smith looked away.

"His name is Charles," Heather said. "Charles Neal."

"I'm well aware," Caleb replied.

"Then use it," Heather said. Her tone was firm.

"You got it. Which one of you would like to go first with Coach Charles Neal?"

Heather Ward marched forward. Caleb handed her the branding iron.

Duncan Ward was apparently not keen on waiting for his turn and immediately retrieved the second branding iron from the fire. Caleb did not have to give them the go-ahead to start when they were ready; they had already begun in earnest.

4

Finished, Charles Neal's body had been branded head to toe. Duncan had even branded the man on his forehead, Heather the man's genitals (though that result was a more difficult read given the man's size, Caleb had added to himself privately, once again chomping down onto the inside of his cheek to keep from laughing).

And just as before, after their shared beating of the man, the couple had retreated into the corner to cry into one another's arms.

Caleb took this moment to retrieve a small handheld mirror from his backpack and squatted before Charles Neal. The man continued to writhe and moan in agony, oblivious to Caleb's—he couldn't help himself now—grin looming over him.

Caleb snapped his fingers in front of Charles Neal's face. "Charles," he said. "Hey, Coach Charles, look at me." Charles Neal did. "Wanna see your new look?"

Charles Neal could only blink back at Caleb.

"I'll take that as a yes." Caleb held the mirror in front of Charles Neal's face so he could see the brand Duncan Ward had given him between both eyes, the brands Heather Ward had given him on his right and left cheek. "Nice, huh? All things considered, I think they did good work."

Charles Neal shut his eyes tight.

"No?" Caleb said. And then it occurred to him: "Oh shit! It's a mirror!" He started laughing. "You're seeing it *backwards*, aren't you? What is it that you're seeing?" Caleb scooted over on his butt and propped Charles Neal's head up close to his own so they could both get a good look in the mirror. Caleb barked out a solitary laugh the second he saw it.

"*Odep!* Fucking says *odep!* Sounds like the name of a Greek god or something, doesn't it? Or no, wait; how about we use Hotep? You ever heard of the word Hotep, Charles? It's Egyptian. Means to be at peace. You at peace, Charles?" He gestured over towards the Wards. "Think they're at peace? I reckon no, despite what they just did. Those people will never be at peace, Charles—because of you."

Caleb pulled his cell phone from his pocket, snapped a photo of Charles Neal's face, and then showed it to him. "That better, Charles?" he said. "What do you think? Think that's accurate?" Once again Charles Neal shut his eyes tight.

Caleb turned towards the Wards. "Don't worry, I'll delete it. Unless you want a copy?"

"We just might," Duncan Ward said.

Still on board.

Caleb could scarcely contain his joy.

"Okey-dokey, coach," Caleb said, patting Charles Neal on one of the seeping brands on his chest, Charles Neal moaning right after. "I'd say it's about time for the final whistle."

Caleb hopped to his feet and went to his backpack again. He produced a Glock 17 TB with a five-inch suppressor. Caleb had recently used the same gun—and, more notably, its five-inch suppressor—to sodomize a fat piece of human-trafficking shit before pulling the trigger endless times.

He handed the gun to the Wards, waiting for one of them to take it.

"It won't make much noise," Caleb said. "Safety is off, and it's fully loaded. All you have to do is pull the trigger. I'll call one of my cleaners once you're on the road. There'll be zero traces. It'll be as though he literally vanished off the face of the earth."

Heather and Duncan Ward took turns until the gun was empty.

5

Doylestown, Pennsylvania

Caleb's relationship with his psychologist, Dr. Audrey Flynn, was an unusual one, to say the least. To put it bluntly, Dr. Flynn fucked Caleb to keep his violent urges at bay.

Sitting now in the driveway of Dr. Flynn's home—his therapy was always conducted in her home, for obvious reasons—Caleb reflected on past sessions (the subject was hardly a virgin) that summed up the nature of their unorthodox therapy.

He did this often, this reflection, for as beneficial as the therapy was to his psyche, it *did* tug at something inside that left him feeling weak, as though he was not strong enough to handle such issues on his own.

And so this reflection had come to be the norm for Caleb. To justify his sitting in an idling car outside Dr. Flynn's home office, waiting to go inside, knowing damn well that he would not be fantasizing about the good doctor as he fucked her, sexy as she was, but about what he'd conducted at the Wards'. The blissful atrocity of it all. His need for sexual release following such atrocities.

And even though upon this reflection he would always feel a bit better, grant him the justification that allowed him to go on for another day as is, Caleb felt it was akin to how an addict rationalized still using because it warded off sickness from withdrawal—nothing but self-serving bullshit. The addict could quit if they really wanted to. All the justification in the world—and Caleb was guilty of quite a bit—was just more heaping bowls of that self-serving bullshit.

And wasn't that what he was? An addict? Caleb had never bought the whole theory about addiction being a disease, something out of the addict's control, but right now such a theory sounded just fine to him. The driveway of Dr. Flynn's may as well have been the parking lot outside a liquor store, Dr. Flynn's home the store itself. Caleb in his car telling himself he'd had a bad day and *deserved* a fucking drink. He was not weak. He was simply wired wrong, to no fault of his own.

And there *was* some truth to this. A truth that Caleb clung to like a life raft at sea. He had not been born an addict, as addicts so often claim, he had been *made* one. How could that possibly be his fault? Why *shouldn't* he go into the store and buy that bottle so he could get his fix? It wasn't his fucking fault, dammit.

So Caleb continued to reflect on those past sessions, as he'd done countless times before, so that he might then leave his car and stroll right on into that store and buy the bottle that was Dr. Flynn's body as blameless as one could be in their doing:

"You know about the expression 'taking one for the team'?" Dr. Flynn had asked him.
"Yeah," Caleb had replied.
"Well, that's what I do with you."
"What team are you taking one for?"

> *"Humanity."*
> *"Humanity?"*
> *"Correct."*
> *"I don't think I follow,"* he'd said.
> *"It's nothing we haven't covered before, Caleb. Same song, just a different version."*
> *"Why a different version?"*
> *"Why the need to constantly hear the same song?"*

Oh, how true this was.

> *"You're the shrink; you tell me."*
> *"I already know."*
> *"It's not guilt,"* he'd said. *"I feel no guilt for what I do."*
> *"I never once suggested otherwise. I think you feel guilt for the after."*
> *"The after?"*
> *"After we fuck."*
> *"I actually enjoy that part quite a bit."*
> *"After* we fuck.*"*

Caleb remembered being stumped by what she'd been insinuating. Dr. Flynn went on.

> *"Clearly, the same answer to the same question isn't working for you. I need to offer you a different perspective. I won't be your enabler, Caleb. I won't tell you what you want to hear just so you can sleep at night."*

He remembered feeling both frustration and admiration for Dr. Flynn's ability to do her job with such detached precision, and that detached precision had never once changed. It would surely be no different today. She would spread her legs for him, and despite her performance, or even any pleasure she might have derived from the act, it was purely physical. Purely clinical. Nothing else. And Caleb, being the man he was at the end of the day, having the ego all men possessed, often struggled with this. He often hoped there was at least *something* behind that clinical way about her. That she perhaps enjoyed their sessions on some level or another.

Only Dr. Flynn, in all her aptitude, had never once led on to such a thing. She was constant ice, never once allowing any warmth Caleb might try to throw her way to thaw her in the slightest so that it may appeal to his ego.

"Tell me what you meant about taking one for the team. For humanity," he'd said.

"As you well know, you were my patient before you left Bucks County. Our sessions were productive, yet you obviously needed more, hence your sudden up and leaving to pursue the training in what would later become your vocation. You returned to me years later, desperate. Your previous doctor during your time away had tried chemically castrating you; a last resort in a bid to reduce your urges. It helped, but not without its impressive list of cons, yes?

"I started to grow tits. My dick was useless. I sweat constantly. My depression became horrific."

Caleb remembered the need to reiterate his lack of guilt in the vocation that he'd chosen…or that had chosen him.

"I only take lives that need taking."
"That you deem need taking."
"Seriously? A pedophile-piece-of-shit human trafficker? You

> *believe the world is a better place with him in it?"*
> *"Of course not. But you are walking a fine line."*
> *"How's that?"*
> *"How soon until the wicked become the mildly wicked? The mildly wicked the occasional offender? Playing judge, jury, and executioner is a slippery slope. Much like the addict who begins sporadically, how soon until they find a reason to use for every occasion to justify their needs?"*

Ah yes—*her* use of the addict analogy. But who was he kidding? Dr. Flynn had patented the damned analogy from session one, and he'd happily borrowed it from then on out. Only her version served as a warning; Caleb's version, an excuse.

> *"Won't happen to me," he'd said.*
> *"Said every addict who ever lived."*
> *"It won't. I will never become what I despise."*
> *"So you say. But like all addicts who wish to stop, they can't do it alone. Which is why we're here, in my bed, your cock still slick with 'therapy.'"*
> *"Is this the part where you finally tell me what taking one for the team means?"*
> *"I was hoping you would have pieced it together by now."*

Caleb remembered having done so. Sort of. However, be it shame to speak it aloud himself, or the fact that he'd wanted to hear it from Dr. Flynn in a more clinical fashion (sometimes layman's terms weren't better), Caleb had felt unsure about taking a stab at it. He'd felt comfortable enough with a proposed volley, though, something often done in their sessions together.

> *"I'll start," he'd said.*
> *"All right then."*

"My sexual desires are...?"
"Fueled by the macabre."
"To no fault of my own?"
"Correct. But it's there all the same. Already programmed. Already hard-wired. You experienced great violence during crucial formative years in your life. When most boys were innocently masturbating, you were beating a man to death with a baseball bat in self-defense. And never mind what you SAW during those formative years."
"So, like a..."

He remembered pausing, the words—or *the* word—to come all but choking him.

"...like a serial killer, sex and violence for me are intertwined."
"Correct. When you kill, you think about fucking. When you fuck, you think about killing."
"I still feel like we're going in circles. None of this is new to either of us."
"Better you fuck me than someone else."

Caleb remembered immediately getting her innuendo, the double entendre that "fuck" held in the exchange.

"I only hurt bad people."
"Yes, but as we just discussed, your desire to hurt is at one with your lust. Despite good intentions, a slipup is exceptionally probable."
"So, your pussy keeps my dick from hurting good people."

Yes. *Yes*, that was it. That was goddamn right. All the justification and clarification he needed for now. Caleb exited his car and went inside to get that bottle.

6

Only there would be no bottle today—only a sippy cup. Dr. Flynn had suggested weaning.

"We've tried that already," Caleb said. "It didn't work."

"Which is why we're going to try again."

They were seated across from each other in Dr. Flynn's home office. No desk between them. Dr. Flynn did not care for desks between her and her patients. She believed such a practice produced more of negative power dynamic as opposed to a shared one, a more productive one.

"Why?" Caleb asked.

"It was always the plan, Caleb." Dr. Flynn, mid-forties, was exceptionally attractive. The only thing more attractive was her manner; Caleb believed she would have been equally cool and collected in a foxhole as she was here in her office.

"I know that, but…" He had nothing. And he felt a stab of shame. Felt like a kid with no good reply who might soon resort to whining or, worse yet, begging.

"But what?"

"But we tried that already." *Really? Just going to repeat yourself? Sad.*

And of course when Dr. Flynn repeated herself in her clinical yet reassuring way, it was anything but sad. "Which is why we're going to try again." She smiled with her eyes. Dr. Flynn rarely smiled with anything else.

Caleb was direct, if not crass. "So then what? You going to give me a blowjob?"

Dr. Flynn gave a long, solitary blink. Refined patience. "I could, if you like."

"It won't be the same."

"Hence the aim of therapy. No competent therapist strives for routine with their patients."

"What if it still doesn't work?"

"Won't know unless we try. Come on, Caleb, were you really planning on this unorthodox treatment of ours to last forever?"

"No," he immediately replied, but didn't mean it. "I mean…I don't know. Why not?"

"Because it was never our goal," she reiterated. "What were you planning to do when I retired?"

"You're in your forties. You planning on retiring soon?"

"From our special brand of therapy? Yes. Would you honestly want to keep doing this when I'm in my seventies?"

"You look thirty. When you're seventy, you'll look sixty. Probably fucking fifty. I'm good with that." *Dude, stop. Just stop.*

Dr. Flynn gave the long, solitary blink again.

"I'm sorry," Caleb said. "I just—I wasn't expecting this. Not today. A little heads-up would have been nice."

"If I'd given you a heads-up, would you have shown?"

"Of course I would have."

"But would you have really shown?" She tapped her index finger against the side of her head and then pointed at his. "Or would you have been detached, almost better if you hadn't shown at all?"

Caleb looked out Dr. Flynn's office window and said nothing for a spell. A silent yielding to her truth. How many times had he looked out that window over the years?

When he finally faced her again, the crass dummy on his shoulder fired off another blurt before his better judgment could snuff it. "So what's the endgame then? Sex doll?"

"Actually, that's not a bad suggestion."

"I was kidding."

"Yes, I'm aware. Your tact is often as opaque as polished glass. Still, I would like the endgame to be some form of self-fulfillment, be it yourself or a prop of some kind."

"Hmmm…wonder why Bundy and Gacy never thought of that."

"Because they enjoyed satiating their impulses. You resent yours."

Caleb's sarcasm followed by Dr. Flynn's immediate—and fitting—response had him looking out the window again. He eventually sighed and brought his attention back on her. "So, what do we do now?"

"You mentioned a blowjob."

The two studied one another like buyer and seller at an open market, only there would be no haggling in this exchange. The proprietor was immovable in her offer, and Caleb read it all too well. This was it. Take it or leave it.

And Caleb, as one did when the price was too steep, yet the need to have was too strong, took it.

―――

THEY DID NOT ADJOURN to the bedroom. Dr. Flynn blew Caleb right where he sat. And goddamn if it wasn't fucking wonderful.

Though he wasn't about to admit that to her anytime soon.

7

Caleb dissected his most recent session with Dr. Flynn on the drive back to his office. He felt guilty for his behavior. Or was shameful the more appropriate word? Both were kind of the same, and thus both fit the bill.

No, wait—let's add one more in there, he thought. *Pathetic.*

He felt guilty, shameful, and pathetic, and if his office had been a longer drive, he would have assuredly come up with a few more goodies to tack on to the existing three.

For now, pathetic held the most weight of those three. For someone who prided himself on discipline and code, Caleb had embodied pathetic all too well when Dr. Flynn had informed him of her intentions to wean him. And as much as he'd hoped when first backing out of her driveway that she might go back on her intentions in future sessions, now, after five minutes in the car, he wasn't so sure.

The blowjob had been epic, both physically *and* therapeutically. Sure, she'd given him head before—and it was always good—but it had always been foreplay; he knew sex was to follow. And if he could beat the dead-horse analogy about the addict getting his fix to death once more, sometimes the knowledge that you had your next fix secured was just as important as the current fix you held in your hand.

Today, he knew there would be no fix after the blowjob. And while it worried him at the time, he felt all right about it for now. It had nothing to do with getting his rocks off, either. The blowjob on its own seemed to have served its purpose. Quenched his need for release after violence. Maybe he could do this after all, this weaning thing, the endgame that was self-gratification. He was tired of being weak, tired of being the addict with all the hollow justifications. Maybe he could make it work. He sure as hell planned to try.

The sex doll thing was too creepy for his liking, though. He'd stick to jerking off when the time came.

8

Newtown, Pennsylvania

Caleb's office was on the second floor of a modest building, "Hudson and Russell Investment" stamped on the office door.

They never got any patrons looking for financial advice.

Caleb entered and saw what he saw almost every day when first entering his office:

He saw Nick Chapman at the front desk, fielding inquiries on both his laptop and cell phone.

He saw Thomas and Faye Rose, his tech team, seated across from one another, one larger desk over, their desk with considerably more laptops, considerably more of everything needed to ensure Caleb's assignments went as smoothly as ever, that he would never have to go into a job blind, that he would know every conceivable entry and exit point, every conceivable bit of intel necessary to get the job done as efficiently as possible. They hadn't let him down yet.

They were as close to a family as you could get, the four of them (cleaners and personal doctor not included, being the subcontractors they were), and Caleb felt something akin to love for all three, as he believed they felt for him, but there was always a line. Always something unspoken that would never allow all four to truly love. They knew who Caleb was, his backstory. They *certainly* knew what he did for a living. He was the feral cat you kept in the barn to deal with rats. You fed the cat, admired its ability to eradicate, grew to have great fondness for it, but never forgot the unpredictable nature of it when you got too close.

And Caleb was fine with that. He would prefer admiration for his capabilities and respect for his unpredictable nature over true familial love. The former allowed his team to excel at their job, never forgetting that it *was* a job. The latter, that familial love, would cloud judgment when things grew difficult, as they often did.

"I'm assuming all went well?" Nick asked Caleb.

"Yep. They wire final payment?"

Nick nodded. "First thing."

Caleb nodded back.

Nick Chapman—mid-thirties, short dark hair, slim, rimless glasses—stood and folded his arms across his chest, a pacifying behavior for his uncertainty in what he was about to ask next. "Did it go exactly as planned?"

Caleb, who had started fixing himself a cup of coffee from the office's corner kitchen, glanced back at Nick with one eyebrow arched. "Meaning what?"

Nick gave a partial shrug. Caleb, who read body language as well as he did English, knew a half-truth was to come from Nick's rise of only one shoulder.

"Just making sure," Nick said.

"Lies make baby Jesus cry, Nick," Caleb said, returning to his coffee.

Faye snorted a quick laugh behind him.

"I'm not lying about anything. I just…I just wanted to know if it went exactly as planned. My heart broke for that family. That kid."

Caleb blew on his coffee and took a sip. "Gee, Nick, if I didn't know any better, I would think this had to do more with morbid curiosity than any sympathy for one of the thousands of clients you've vetted over the years."

Now Thomas snorted.

Nick shot Faye and Thomas a frown. Back to Caleb: "I just wanted to know if—"

"You wanted to know if the client went through with the whole branding iron thing."

Thomas Rose—mid-thirties, short, bald, pale, plump—raised both eyebrows at his wife, Faye. She returned the gesture, an unspoken "this should be good" exchange. Eternally in love, the couple often drew stares in public, and it had nothing to do with their interracial marriage, but more to do with the Haitian-born Faye's beauty in contrast with Thomas's lack thereof. Five inches taller than Thomas, with striking blue eyes contrasting her dark skin, and an exotic accent to boot, Faye drew looks in public whether she was with Thomas or not.

Nick finally succumbed. "Well, did they?"

Caleb took another sip of coffee and turned towards Thomas and Faye. "I think he's beginning to enjoy his work too much."

Thomas and Faye chuckled back, but they were an easy read too; they wanted the goods just as much as Nick.

Caleb relented. "Yes, they went through with it. Has the Manson family gotten their fix now? You guys all good?"

Deep down, Caleb knew their inquisitiveness *was* nothing more than morbid curiosity, something the entire world was guilty of. There was not an evil bone among the three of them. Sure, their jobs facilitated murder, but it was the murder of scum, something the three were at peace with, otherwise Caleb would have booted them on day one.

"And yes, I took photos, and no, you can't see them," Caleb added. He then set his coffee down and extended his hand towards Nick. "What do you got for me?"

Ordinarily, Nick would have handed Caleb files of potential clients. Today he handed him nothing.

"Nothing?" Caleb confirmed.

"Well, yeah there were, but nothing that passed the test."

Caleb's screening process for prospective clients was exceptionally thorough. Though he received monetary compensation for his work, he would not accept just any job; money was, and had always been, a secondary factor.

Too often potential jobs would come across Nick's desk—a husband or wife who wanted the other gone, usually for infidelity or financial reasons; an employee of a high-end firm who wanted their competition eliminated so that they would be next in line for the big promotion; someone with a simple grudge, just to name a few—but Nick always batted them away. A potential target had to make Stalin look like a saint in order to catch Nick's, and thus Caleb's, eye.

"Well, then guess what?" Caleb said. "I'm going to get a drink." He'd been craving one since leaving Dr. Flynn's office, and it had nothing to do with a sort of subliminal implant about the stupid addict analogies. Truth was, he still wanted to mull over what went down today with Dr. Flynn, and a few cocktails while doing so sounded just fine to him right now.

"This early?" Faye asked, though it sounded more like *Dis early*, her Haitian accent having her pronounce th's with d's. "It's like two o'clock."

"Day drinking, my dear," Caleb replied. "One of the few luxuries left in the world." He looked at Nick. "Text me any interesting jobs that might come up."

Nick nodded. "Will do."

Caleb left.

"I think you pissed him off," Thomas said to Nick as he produced a Three Musketeers bar and began unwrapping it.

"He's always pissed off," Nick said.

"He's always pissed off with *you*," Faye said, robotically reaching across the desk and taking the Three Musketeers bar from her husband. "You're too nosy."

Nick frowned again and went back to his desk. Thomas sulked about his candy.

Faye broke off a small piece of the Three Musketeers bar and handed it to her husband. She smiled lovingly at him, which softened the blow.

9

Caleb chose an Applebee's, roughly a five-minute drive from the office. He figured that at two o'clock in the afternoon, on a weekday, he might have the place to himself.

He was more than a little disappointed to find out this was not the case. The place was surprisingly full, with the most prominent of the patrons lining the circular bar being three well-fed men in pricey suits and jewelry carrying on as if they were at an Irish wedding reception. And to those who might not know any better, perhaps they were. Or perhaps they were three businessmen who'd chosen to drink their lunch instead of eating it. They certainly stood out from the rest of the patrons at the bar—red-nosed men and women with leather skin, feeding their habit—and it wasn't because of their volume, but by the arrogance with which they carried themselves.

And that arrogance had nothing to do with liquid courage. Because Caleb *did* know better. He immediately made them for the organized criminals they were. What the heck they were doing in an Applebee's in a sleepy little town in Bucks County was the only thing Caleb didn't know.

Nor did he care. Still, their raucous behavior *did* bother Caleb, so he chose a stool as far away from the three as he could. He'd even contemplated leaving at first, finding a quiet dive instead, but he had no intentions of staying long. He was here now. So be it.

The bartender—an older woman with the tired appearance of someone who'd been in the service industry one year too many—approached Caleb and placed a laminated menu before him. Caleb slid it back.

"Just here for drinks," he said. The bartender smiled an "I get it" smile, and asked him what he wanted. Actually, she asked him what his predilection was, which Caleb found amusing. One year too many or not, she still had the charm.

"Jack neat and Miller Lite bottle, please," Caleb said.

"Only got Miller Lite on draft," she said.

Caleb didn't like draft beer. Too often the staff didn't wash the glasses completely free of that blue crap they dunked it in to sterilize. He didn't mind visiting the restroom for a leak, but because his stomach needed a leak? No thanks.

"Coors Light?" Caleb asked.

"Can do," she said.

The bartender returned with his order. Caleb sipped the warm Jack and then chased it with the frosty beer. The comforting burn in his chest was almost immediate, and he let out a pleased sigh.

Then it all went to hell when one of the men in the pricey suits slapped a waitress's ass.

10

Caleb immediately left his stool and approached the three men. "You don't do shit like that," he said to them.

All three laughed in Caleb's face.

"And who the fuck are you, tough guy?" the shortest of the three asked. It was always the shortest who had the biggest mouth. He also happened to be the one who'd slapped the waitress's ass. Napoleon in the flesh.

"Someone who doesn't sit on the sidelines and watch, or, God forbid, film it with their fucking phone."

The short suit pulled a face. "A *what?*"

Caleb said nothing. The waitress who'd been violated had since retreated towards the other end of the bar, visibly shaken, yet still looking on.

Another suit spoke up. "Listen, big fella, it would be in your best interest to go on back to your stool. You don't wanna be a fucking hero with us."

"Clearly you know nothing about one's best interest," Caleb said. "If you did, you'd have left by now."

All three laughed again. "Clearly *you* know nothing about who you're fucking with," the third suit—the biggest of the three—said.

"Oh no, I've got a pretty good idea," Caleb said. "The fancy suits, the excessive jewelry, the bellies on all three of you that suggest you couldn't run a quarter of a mile without dropping dead from a fucking heart attack…and yet you throw your weight around—pun intended, by the way—because experience has told you that no one ever dares fight back after being informed of who they're"—he made air quotes with both his hands—"'fucking with.'"

"If you know," the short suit said, "then you've got bigger balls than brains, tough guy."

"Guilty," Caleb said. "I ran out of fucks to give about people like you a long time ago."

"Is that right?"

"It is. Here's what I want to happen now," Caleb began, "and you can stop that," he said to the big suit creeping up on his left, "you might as well be wearing a fucking bell."

The big suit looked genuinely surprised that Caleb spotted his intentions of a sucker punch. He crept no further.

"So, here's what I want to happen now," Caleb said again. "I want you to apologize to the waitress you assaulted, and then I want you to give her a generous tip for her troubles. Think you can do that?"

Two of the suits laughed again, but the short one did not. Instead, he turned and faced the two suits and began patting the air. "No, no—tough guy's right; I was out of line, I was out of line." He looked over at the waitress by the other end of the bar. "Hey, sweetheart," he called to her, "sweetheart, come on over here."

Surprisingly, the waitress did. She stayed a cautious few feet away, though.

"No, no, come on—*here*," the short suit said, pointing to a spot by his feet. "It's all right."

The waitress moved closer.

"I would like to take this moment to apologize for my earlier behavior. I have no excuse." He pulled a thick wad of bills from his coat pocket, snaked out a hundred dollar bill, and then held it in front of her face so she could clearly see the denomination. "This is for you."

The waitress tentatively went to take the bill, but the short suit stuffed it down the front of her shirt before she could.

The other two suits laughed yet again. The waitress slapped a hand over her chest and stumbled back.

The short suit turned back towards Caleb. "Happy now, tough guy—"

Caleb hammered his right fist onto the point of the short one's chin, putting him to sleep before he hit the floor. Drove a left and then another right into the jaws of two and three—one for each. They too were snoring before they hit the deck. The biggest of the three even crumpled on top of the littlest. Caleb found that insanely hilarious, but did not smile.

The patrons—and not a single one wasn't watching at this point—gave what amounted to be a collective gasp. The waitress looked on in disbelief. Didn't stop her from plucking the hundred from the inside of her shirt and slipping it into her back pocket, though.

Caleb pulled a fifty from his own back pocket and laid it on the bar. "I should probably go," he said to the bartender.

"Probably a good idea," the bartender replied.

Shame, Caleb thought. Her charm, and now her composed wit after such a scene, would have made for decent conversation here and there during his stay.

Caleb picked up his Jack neat and finished it in a gulp. Add Applebee's to the list of places he probably shouldn't frequent anymore. At least this one. His own fault, though. Shitting where you eat and all that.

"Spend it well," he said to the waitress as he walked past her and left.

———

On the drive back to his apartment, Caleb wondered whether he'd hear something about what he'd done, and it had nothing to do with the police.

11

The second Caleb entered his apartment he was blitzed by Rosco, and it had nothing to do with needing to go outside for a número uno or dos. His master was home, and it was time to get their cuddle on.

Despite recent events, Caleb happily obliged—someone could remove his arms and legs and Caleb would still find a way to get their cuddle on, undeterred—dropping to the floor and rolling around with his dog, rough-housing, smooching, singing the stupid songs one does to their pets, ridiculous lyrics on repeat and all:

"*He's the Rosco boy!—the Rosco boy!—the Roscoey-ist of the Rosco boyyyys!*" Then a brief pause for more rough-housing and love before: "Oh, yes, he is, yes, he is, *he's the Rosco boy!—the Rosco boy!—the Roscoey-ist of the Rosco boyyys!*"

Rosco ate it all up in his way with squeaks and chirps and whines and licks, body vibrating, little tail going a zillion miles an hour.

Song finished—mercifully, to those who might have been unfortunate enough to be listening—Caleb rolled onto his side and began scratching Rosco under his chin as he spoke. "What did my boy get up to while I was gone, huh? What did my boy get up to while I was gone? Did you give those squirrels a talking-to through the sliding glass door? Yes? Did you give those squirrels a talking-to through the sliding glass door while I was gone?" Song or no song, the repeat would never die, nor would the shit-talking squirrels. They were legion in their quest to drive Rosco nuts—park, home, wherever.

"Your daddy got up to some stuff today," Caleb went on. "Stupid stuff, but stuff that needed doing. Pretty sure they were just wannabe wiseguys, but you never can tell these days. Fingers crossed it doesn't amount to anything worth worrying about. Best-case scenario is the police come knocking, though if those guys were actually who they hinted they were, I doubt they'll press any charges. Be interesting to see if someone else comes knocking. Actually, would be interesting to see if they could even locate which door to come knocking *on*."

Caleb stood and went into his kitchen for a glass of water. Rosco followed, hoping water wasn't the only thing Caleb would be getting from the kitchen.

And it wasn't; Caleb retrieved a biscuit from the doggy-designed cookie jar on his counter and dropped it at Rosco's feet, his mind going over his recent words to his dog as he filled a glass from the faucet.

Could they find him if they wanted to? He wasn't exactly the easiest guy to locate. He'd paid in cash, and did not frequent that particular Applebee's often; no one knew his name. He seldom gave his real name to strangers anyway.

Cameras. Surely the place had cameras. *Every* place had cameras these days, never mind the patrons and their phones. Or should he now refer to them as witnesses? To his surprise, there had been quite a few witnesses on a weekday afternoon. And despite his show of chivalry in defending the waitress, the odds of all those patrons being tight-lipped once the police arrived were slim. Perhaps one, who did not approve of his chivalry, the violent means with which he went about it (the world being the pussified place it was these days), even had the presence of mind to catch his license plate as he drove off, if not the aforementioned CCTV cameras should one or two be perched in the parking lot somewhere.

Caleb finished his water and set the empty glass on the counter. He really didn't know what to expect. Part of him didn't care. He had no regrets about what he'd done, and he'd certainly dealt with his share of threats in his day, many of them connected to all sorts of organized crime. The real truth was that he simply found it easier not to ruminate over the whole damn thing.

Rosco whined at his feet. Caleb looked down at his dog. He knew what that specific whine meant. Not another biscuit, but número uno or dos time, and step on it.

Caleb fetched Rosco's collar and took him outside for a walk. When he came back inside an hour later, flopped on the sofa, and clicked on the TV, his first words were: "Ahhhh *shit*."

12

The incident had only been a few hours ago, but the media was already doing their parasite thing. Not only was Caleb's incident at Applebee's being broadcast, but the damn thing *had* been filmed, and with solid clarity to boot. And who had filmed the encounter? CCTV cameras inside the restaurant? Nope. It had been some asshole sitting on the sidelines, filming with his goddamn phone. Fucking technology; it could be your greatest ally or your worst enemy.

The piece did not paint Caleb in a bad light, however. On the contrary, while technology had been his enemy in showcasing his separating the three dickheads from their consciousness, it had been his ally in showing the incidents leading up to it. They had missed the slap on the waitress's ass, but had started filming right after, when Caleb had confronted the three men, catching the shoving of the hundred dollar bill down the front of the waitress's shirt. Couple this footage with the footage of the patrons who were all too keen to be interviewed for their five minutes of fame (some mentioning the slap on the ass), praising Caleb for his coming to the waitress's aid, and he did indeed come off in a decent light.

But Caleb didn't care about being a hero. What he cared about was his own little action movie being broadcast on a major news outlet, his angry mug clear as day. Further digging from Caleb would show his same angry mug on *several* news outlets, multiple social media platforms to boot. Someone had already even spliced the fight footage to fitting music, displayed it in regular speed and then slow-mo before uploading it to all the trendy platforms, where it was clearly on its way to becoming viral.

"*Fuuuuuck...*" Caleb said, slapping his laptop shut. Rosco, who had been sawing toothpicks next to Caleb on the couch, flicked his head up when the laptop's lid snapped shut. Caleb looked at Rosco. "This...this is not good, brother."

Or maybe it wasn't so bad. From the multiple pieces Caleb had viewed, his identity had not been revealed, nor had the identities of the three men he'd dropped. Some outlets had even blurred the faces of the three (curiously, not his own, though; perhaps they wrongly thought he *wanted* to be Superman for a day).

This lack of identity for all three, including Caleb's own, was definitely a good thing, wasn't it? For Caleb it sure as hell was; he definitely had no desire to play Superman for a day, his current position with "Hudson and Russell Investment" operating that much better under anonymity and all.

The bad guys? Caleb presumed that it was a good thing for them too. And while their reasons for it being a good thing shared similarities with Caleb's—anonymity—there was a stark contrast in the desire for that anonymity.

Shame and reprisal.

If these three assholes really were wiseguys, then they would want anonymity in order to save face. Shame.

And if these three assholes really were wiseguys, then they

would want anonymity in order to deliver some payback without eyes on them. Reprisal.

Caleb wasn't fond of that last reason.

13

A vast office, tastefully decorated. Antiques and art. On the far left wall hung a flat screen TV the size of a small garage door. The TV was on. It was showcasing a segment on something that had transpired at an Applebee's in Bucks County, Pennsylvania.

A man, immaculately dressed, sat behind an excessive desk at the far end of the office, watching the segment. Three men stood before the great desk, watching the same segment, their collective faces angry.

When the segment on the TV ended, the man behind the desk pointed his remote and killed the broadcast, the room darkening. The man then proceeded to pour himself a whiskey from a crystal decanter. He sipped the whiskey slowly. He did not allow eye contact with the three men just yet.

"Who wants to begin?" the man behind the desk asked, still affording no eye contact with the three.

"Fucking asshole," the shortest of the three men said.

"Are you referring to yourselves, or the man who knocked all three of you cold with one shot?"

"Huh?"

The man behind the desk finally gave them his full attention. Handsome, mid-fifties, salt and pepper hair smartly parted to one side, the man said: "True, you are not the best and brightest in our outfit, but I'd like to think that even you knew what I was insinuating."

"No, it wasn't like that, boss. That there"—the short man pointed at the TV—"that was a smear job. We were just having a little fun, when fucking John Wayne comes over and cheap-shots us."

"Had we no footage, I would have truly believed that was how you remembered it. But of course we do have the footage. So, is that the story you'd still prefer to tell?"

Another of three chimed in. "We told him who we were. Told him it would be in his best interest to let us be. But this fucking guy, he wouldn't budge. Seen one too many tough-guy movies, if you ask me."

The man sipped more whiskey. "Well, if you ask me, it looks as if he's done more than just *seen* his share of tough-guy movies."

The second man looked at his feet.

"And when you told this John Wayne who you were, what exactly did you tell him?" the man behind the desk asked.

"Nothing specific," the tallest of the three said. "It's just like Franky said; we told him it would be in his best interest to leave us be. That's the God's honest truth."

The man behind the desk nodded slowly. "I see." He stood, flattened out his suit, and adjusted his tie. He then produced three more glasses and filled them from the crystal decanter. He beckoned them closer.

All three tentatively approached. Neither of the three took the whiskeys presented to them just yet.

The man stepped out from behind the desk and got close. "What would you guess my mood is right now?"

"Pissed off?" the shortest offered.

"At whom?"

"John Wayne. You want some payback, yeah? We'll be more than happy to make it right, boss."

The man laughed softly. "Yes, you appeared more than capable the first time."

"This'll be different," the short one said. "We'll pay him a visit and catch him off-guard. We'll show him you can't disrespect—"

The man held up a hand, cutting the short one off. "*I* will be paying him a visit. And do not—for one second—lecture me about respect. Your actions today clearly indicate your grasp of the subject."

"We didn't hurt the girl or anything," the short one said. "Hell, I gave her a fucking Benjamin, after all."

The man's eyebrows rose. "Oh, you did, did you? Was that what you shoved down her shirt?"

The short one nodded back. "Probably the biggest tip she got all week at a fucking Applebee's." He had the audacity to laugh after his quip.

The other two nervously laughed along. The man soon joined them, gesturing towards their drinks. The short one reached first. The man stopped laughing, grabbed the letter opener on his desk, and rammed it into the short one's hand, pinning it to the desk.

The short one cried out and dropped to his knees, hand staying put on the desk, the letter opener serving as a fine anchor.

The other two took a giant step back.

The man calmly reached into his breast pocket, produced a wad of bills, plucked a hundred free, and shoved it into the shorter one's screaming mouth. He then jerked the letter opener free of the short one's pinned hand, the short one then falling onto his back, clutching his bloodied hand and choking on the hundred dollar bill.

The man fingered the bloodied hole he'd made in his desk and looked displeased about the imperfection. He glanced up at the other two. "Shall I make it all okay with a 'Benjamin' for you two as well?"

They immediately collected the short one and ushered him out of the office.

The man took his spot behind the desk again, finished his glass of whiskey, and made a phone call.

14

Still on the sofa, Caleb looked down at Rosco. Rosco looked up at him.

"How much you wanna bet Nick, Thomas, and Faye saw all that shit and will be calling any second now?" he said.

Rosco started wagging his tail after his master's query. Wagged his tail after every word his master spoke. Pavlov had his bell that made dogs salivate, Caleb had his voice that made his dog's tail go nuts.

Caleb scratched the top of his dog's head. Rosco rolled his head and licked Caleb's hand.

"Yeah," Caleb said, "better to explain everything in person. Maybe I can get there before Nick—and we know it'll be Nick, don't we?—calls. Hold down the fort while I head back to the office?"

Wag, wag, wag.

"You love your dad?"

Wag, wag, wag.

"Maybe some Bacon Buddies when I get back?"

Full-on assault. Wag, lick, whine, nuzzle. Rosco had learned "bacon" before his own name.

Caleb laughed, pried Rosco off, went to get him a few Bacon Buddies now instead of later, but much to Rosco's disappointment, Caleb's vibrating phone on the coffee table stopped his journey.

Caleb looked at his phone. The name "Secretary" came up on his caller ID. He smirked. Nick did not like being referred to as a secretary. Preferred the term "facilitator." The very moment Nick had informed Caleb of this, Caleb changed Nick's caller ID from "Nick" to "Secretary." The little things in life…

"What's up?" Caleb answered.

"Caleb, we just saw what happened," Nick said. "What, uh… what *did* happen?"

"On my way back to the office. I'll tell you there."

Caleb hung up, gave Rosco a few Bacon Buddies from their colorful bag—a cartoon dog, who actually kind of looked like Rosco, frying up a pan of bacon strips—in the pantry, and told him to hold down the fort again.

Rosco barely acknowledged him this time. Bacon would always be a formidable mistress.

15

Back at the office, Caleb told them.

"You think they're connected to anyone significant?" Thomas asked.

"They hinted as much, but I'm not a hundred percent sure," Caleb said. "At first I thought they were. Then I thought they were wannabes. Now I really don't know. The way they were carrying on, though; if they were connected to anyone, they were low-level."

"Why?" Nick asked.

"The way they were throwing their weight around and harassing the staff in a freaking Applebee's on a weekday? No higher-up of any outfit would do that. No midlevel either. It would be like us changing the sign on our door to 'We Kill Assholes Inc.' or whatever. No one with an operation worth hiding advertises in plain sight."

All three nodded in agreement.

"So what does this mean?" Faye asked. *Dis* for *this*.

"What does what mean?"

"What will you do?" Faye elaborated.

"Wait until I hear something, I guess."

"From the police?"

"If I hear anything, I doubt it would be from the police. The identities of the three guys weren't revealed, and believe me, I dug."

"We dug too," Thomas said. "And you're right, no mention of their identities anywhere."

"Then either they woke up and got the hell out of there before the police arrived, or they told them zip when they did," Caleb said. "If they really are connected, then you know how those guys are; they hate the police. If they want something sorted out, they handle it themselves."

"Then this could be a problem," Nick said.

"If they can find me."

"If they're connected to anyone with weight, then it's something worth worrying about. You're an internet star right now. My ten-year-old niece could probably find you."

"Fuck 'em."

"Caleb."

"*Nick.*"

"What if they find *us*?"

"In all our years together, have I ever let anything happen to you guys?"

All three said nothing. While what Caleb said was true, there was always a first for everything, and their collective faces showed it.

Caleb nodded. "Fine—until this thing gets sorted out, you're all officially on vacation. Don't pack a big bag, though; I really don't think it'll amount to much." Truth be told, Caleb wasn't entirely sure about this, but his desire to ease their minds felt paramount.

"What if you need us?" Faye asked.

"Like you've never done anything for me on the road? Go, get lost, all of you. Once whatever might happen happens, I'll let you know."

"Not if you run out of birthdays, you won't," Faye said.

"If they *are* able to find out who I am, then they'd be nuttier than squirrel shit"—lots of squirrel talk lately—"to do anything about it. I'll end each and every one of them."

"This isn't like you," Faye said. "You never talk so tough."

This was true. What started as a try at easing their minds had quickly degenerated into clichéd movie drivel that hurt his own ears.

Caleb chose to ignore her comment and simply reiterated: "Vacation, starting now."

16

Caleb never did get the fill of drinks he'd been after earlier, so he stopped off at a liquor store on the way home and bought a bottle of Jack Daniels. He had no intentions of getting drunk tonight, as he needed to be sharp, but sometimes just the right number of cocktails *did* make his mind sharp. Allowed him to make connections when his brain was inhibited by complete sobriety and the second-guessing that accompanied it.

This was typically not his way. Caleb was no detective. There was no case here to solve. He was a hunter, his team providing all the sleuthing *for* him before he took down his prey. So, why did he feel a need for connections? Crazily enough, he didn't know. It was more a feeling than anything else. Something in his gut. And when Caleb's gut had something brewing but was not quite ready to serve, it was sometimes helpful to add a few libations to the pot. Give it that kick.

So, when Caleb entered his apartment again with his bottle of Jack, and Rosco didn't come running, it all came to him, and it had nothing to do with sleuthing, nor the assistance of the Jack—he hadn't even had any yet, after all—to figure out what his gut had been brewing. It was, in fact, quite simple really.

It had been denial.

Caleb had been uncharacteristically denying his gut for the simple truth that this recent debacle he'd been involved in *was* worth getting his guard up. That it *would* amount to something bigger. Convincing his team that no such thing might occur had been one thing, but denying it to himself, if not just partially? Perhaps it was as simple as to what he'd been musing over earlier: perhaps he simply didn't want the hassle. Admit that his notorious temper had once again bitten off more than it could chew, and that it might, in a foolish bit of hope, go away without bother.

But this was not the case. Rosco refusing to greet him at the door was all the evidence he needed before he entered his living room and saw the three men on his sofa, the one seated on the far left holding Rosco tight.

"Evening," the man in the middle said. He was dressed in a smart black suit, the two men flanking him on the sofa in gray tracksuits.

Caleb didn't return the pleasantry. He instead snapped his fingers and said: "Rosco, come."

Rosco wiggled and whined in the grip of the track-suited man on the left, but the man tightened his hold. Caleb noticed the man's hands. Immediately checked out the hands of the other two, especially the one in the middle, the one in the smart black suit.

"Let go of my dog," Caleb said.

"Relax, John Wick," the man in the black suit replied, "no one's gonna hurt your dog."

"I know," Caleb said.

"How many guesses do you need to figure out why we're here?" the man in the black suit asked.

"None."

"Good—it'll save time."

"The three guys I tuned up today…" Caleb said. "You approve of that behavior?"

"I do not. And believe me, they were reprimanded. I cannot, however, let it go. You see, even if I wanted to, I would soon lose respect and thus control of my crew. We got a code."

"So do I." The men might as well have been dressed in red for all the colors offered to Caleb's vision at that moment.

"So I witnessed," the man in the black suit said. "It was more than a little impressive. Not to mention promising."

Caleb held up the bottle of Jack. "You guys want a drink?"

"Please."

Caleb placed the bottle of Jack on the coffee table before them, turned and retrieved only one glass from the bottom shelf of the small oak bar tucked back in the nook of his living room. He returned and placed the glass before the man on the left holding Rosco. Nothing for the other two, especially the man in the middle, the man in the smart black suit.

Caleb had also retrieved his Glock 42—the 42 being Glock's smallest pistol, ideal for concealability—on that bottom shelf from behind the bar, his movements so swift yet casual as he tucked the small pistol into the back of his waistband that all three men didn't notice until it was too late.

Caleb shot two of the three—the man in the black suit, and the man on the right. One shot each, both dead-center between the eyes. No suppressor on this gun. He prayed his neighbors didn't hear it. Was shocked Rosco didn't bark.

Caleb then aimed the gun at the one seated left, the one holding Rosco, but did not pull the trigger.

"Your hands," Caleb said. "They look soft. You've got a manicure. The other two had chewed nails and lumpy knuckles, presumably from breaking them on heads. Not to mention, try as he might to sound articulate, the one pretending to be in charge still talked like an oaf. Calling me John Wick. 'Gonna' instead of 'going to.' 'Got a' instead of 'have a.' Now let go of my dog."

The man on the left kept his composure, but did as he was told. Rosco ran to Caleb's side and immediately went up on his hind legs. Caleb kept the gun on the man on the left while he reached down to pet Rosco.

The man on the left looked over at the other two. Their heads lay back against the sofa, eyes open, the solitary holes in their heads leaking a stream of blood each.

The man looked back at Caleb, a small smile on the corner of his mouth. "Oh, now I am *very* impressed."

Caleb did not lower the gun. The only reason the man wasn't dead too was: "How did you find me?"

The man waved a hand at Caleb. "Details," he said as though the word irritated him.

"The guy pretending to be you mentioned that I was both impressive *and* promising."

"Indeed. Even more so now."

"Explain." Rosco continued his attempt at climbing Caleb's leg, begging for love. "Rosco, *go!*" Caleb said, snapping his fingers and pointing towards the kitchen. Rosco hopped off his master's leg and did as told. Sounds of Rosco munching dry food from his bowl could be heard seconds later.

"Very adorable dog."

"I know. Explain," Caleb said again.

"May I have that drink now?" The man asked this as though seated at a dinner party, the two dead men next to him dinner guests who were still very much alive.

Caleb gestured with the gun. "Help yourself."

The man leaned forward, unwrapped the plastic from the Jack's top, poured himself a drink, sat back, sipped, and sighed. "Are you a religious man, mister…?"

"You know my name. You found me this quick, then you know my name. Stop fucking around."

The man sipped his whiskey again and smiled. "Fair enough, Caleb. My name is Alexander." Alexander was handsome, mid-fifties, with salt and pepper hair parted smartly to one side.

"Serbian?"

Alexander made a curious face. "No. Why do you ask?"

"I knew a Serbian guy named Alexander, though I'm sure he spelled it differently than you."

"It's not so uncommon a name, Caleb. Funny you would make a Serbian connection without even getting my surname."

"Just brought back a nice memory, is all."

"A friend?"

"No. He was a hired assassin. A man notorious for making pâté out of his victims and serving it to the grieving family at the funeral."

"And that's a fond memory?"

"It is. I made my own pâté out of his right arm and fed it to him."

Alexander looked genuinely amused. "Promising indeed!"

"How's that?"

"Are you a religious man, Caleb?" the man asked again.

"Depends on your definition of religious."

"Do you believe in God?"

"Depends on your definition of God."

Alexander finished the remainder of his whiskey. "How about atonement? Do you believe in that?"

17

"Atonement," Caleb said. "Reparations for an offense of some kind."

"Correct," Alexander said. "And its biblical meaning?"

Caleb didn't reply.

"Let me tell you a story, Caleb."

"*No.* No, no, no—I fucking hate that 'let me tell you a story' shit. I groan whenever some douchebag in the movies does that instead of coming right out with it. So come out with it."

Alexander smiled. "Fair enough. Well, at the risk of upsetting you with anything extensive, I will summarize quickly by saying that atonement is the Catholic practice of confessing one's sins, being given a penance, and then being forgiven and back within God's good graces after carrying out that penance. Do you see a parallel with your definition?"

"I'm not Catholic."

"Nor do you need to be to see a parallel."

"Sounds to me like you're saying I need to be punished for

knocking out your three assholes so God and I can be chums again."

"And should we not add this to your list of sins as well?" Alexander said, gesturing to the two dead associates seated next to him.

"If you can find room. I imagine God has quite the list on me as is."

"Atonement, Caleb. You must atone for your sins. You must make reparations for your offense to us."

"Us who?"

"You'll find that you really don't have much choice in the matter."

"Us who?"

"Would you like to hear your penance now, Caleb?"

"I'd like to put several bullets in your face and be done with all this, Alexander."

"Oh, if only that would make you done with all this. The ceiling to my organization does not end with me; it stretches far, far higher. Look at how quickly *I* found you. In the grand scheme of things, I am not the top rung, Caleb. Do away with me now, and there are rungs above me that would take my place. Rungs that would not be so polite. Rungs that would not offer you a chance at atonement."

Caleb steadied his gun between Alexander's eyes. "You could be bluffing. You could be the top rung. You don't strike me as a foot soldier like your two idiots I just killed."

"Nor am I. Modesty prevents me from going on about my importance within our organization, but rest assured there *are* those far more important than me." He set his empty glass on the coffee table. "My God, Caleb, for someone who loves Rosco as much as you do…"

"Are you threatening my dog?"

"Yes. I'm also threatening all those dear to you."

Caleb thought of his team. More importantly, his mother and sister living under assumed identities in the British Virgin Islands. Could they—whoever the hell *they* were—find them? No one had done so yet. And to say that Caleb had come across a who's who of shady characters in his day would be an understatement.

Was this asshole bluffing? Should he shoot the fucker deader than dead now and see? The guy did have a point. He'd certainly found Caleb quickly enough. No easy task. Couldn't hurt to at least listen to his bullshit atonement thing; it didn't take a genius to figure out that they wanted not him, but something *from* him. Otherwise, they'd have tried to kill him the moment he'd entered his apartment.

Caleb went to the bar and grabbed himself a glass. He filled his and then Alexander's again.

Alexander nodded a polite thank you and sipped.

Caleb gulped his and filled it again. "Go on then. And no fucking stories."

18

Caleb had been right. They did not want him; they wanted something *from* him. And as simple as the request—or demand, the bastards—was, carrying it out would be anything but.

Alexander wanted Caleb to put the kibosh on an upcoming drug deal going down with a rival organization. He'd kept the details intentionally vague for now.

That was it.

And hadn't Caleb thought it would come down to something like that? He was a trained assassin, after all.

But just who the hell were *they*? Much as Caleb would like to think they were nothing he hadn't dealt with before, it unnerved him that they'd found him so quickly. If it had been weeks or even days, fine, but mere hours? And then there was the threat to harm not just Rosco, but those "dear" to him. If they'd found him so quickly, couldn't it at least be possible that they'd locate his team, or, more importantly, his mother and sister in the islands?

He was definitely unnerved. Not to mention pissed the fuck off.

At the end of it, Caleb had asked for twenty-four hours. When Alexander balked at the idea, Caleb reminded him of the two corpses on his sofa, the need to have their bodies attended to. Caleb was not, he emphasized, keen on having them rot in his living room while he followed Alexander off to God knows where for God knows how long.

Alexander had agreed, but not after reminding Caleb—as if he needed any reminding—as to how easily he'd found him if Caleb was planning on using those twenty-four hours to try anything unwise.

As for Caleb's *real* reasoning for those twenty-four hours? He wanted to find out just who the hell Alexander and those "rungs" above him were before he did a damned thing.

He knew exactly where to go, and it had nothing to do with Thomas and Faye.

19

It was a used bookstore in Center City, Philadelphia. The type of place that did not smell of coffee and baked goods as so many modern brick and mortars did, but of old pages well-loved before the curse of technology.

Cats too.

Dylan's Den was home to many cats, yet their presence, their litterboxes were reasonably well-maintained. No offensive odors to overpower the heavenly aroma of those old pages.

Through the tightly packed aisles of books Caleb went. Past the sofas and chairs taken by those who'd decided to read the day away, and towards, not to the front desk just yet, but towards the windowsill to the east of the store. Caleb needed to say hello to Harper first.

Named after the great Harper Lee (all the cats at Dylan's Den were named after famous authors), Harper was a lazy calico who had staked her claim under that east sill for as long as Caleb could remember. The east sill got the most sun, and today was no different, because there Harper lay, dead to the world, and getting her daily fix of vitamin D.

Caleb approached and whispered Harper's name. The calico opened one eye and then closed it again. Caleb took this as permission and felt the sun's warmth on her fur as he stroked the top of her head. Pin-quiet, the store allowed Caleb to hear Harper's purr shortly after. He wondered how she and Rosco would get along.

"Who's a pretty girl?" Caleb whispered as he continued to stroke the top of Harper's head. Harper opened both eyes now before squinting up at Caleb and purring louder. Caleb knew enough about cats to know that while purring was a sign of affection, so was squinting—it was how cats smiled.

And Caleb could not help but smile back before whispering: "See ya soon, pretty girl."

THE MAN behind the front desk was short and thin. Balding, but trying to rock a comb-over. Caleb recognized the man, but the man acted as though he didn't recognize Caleb. This did not surprise Caleb—likely the man *did* recognize him, but there was protocol here.

"Help you?" the clerk asked.

For today's visit, Caleb stated that he was looking for a first edition of *To Kill a Mockingbird*, preferably signed, his buddy Harper sunning on the east sill his inspiration.

The clerk raised an eyebrow. "Are you? Not the easiest of items to locate. Certainly not the cheapest."

"Well aware," Caleb said. He produced a five hundred dollar bill and slid it over to the clerk.

The clerk brought a loupe magnifier to his eye and examined the bill closely. Discontinued and removed from public circulation by the Federal Reserve in 1969, the five hundred dollar bill was in high demand among collectors.

Satisfied, the clerk set the loupe aside and slid the five hundred dollar bill back to Caleb. "Follow me, please."

Left and right through more tightly packed aisles of used books until arriving at a simple door in back that might have been a maintenance closet.

It was not.

Behind that simple door was Dylan of Dylan's Den herself; the room, a modest lounge that was mostly utilitarian despite Dylan's status in her vocation. That vocation? Hardly used books. Dylan had her finger in many pies across the country—none of those pies made of virtue—but what she excelled at was information. Like the mob boss who hardly moved while the consigliere whispered this and that into their ear, so too did Dylan rarely move from her spot in the back of her store.

But there would be no need for whispering in the ear from the clerk upon entrance. Dylan knew Caleb, and she immediately smiled at his arrival.

"Well, if it isn't the Applebee's Avenger," she said as the clerk closed the door behind the three of them.

"Figured you'd heard about that by now."

"Didn't take much doing. You're quite the local celebrity in your little 'burb, aren't you?"

"Unfortunately."

Seated alone at the head of the only table in the room, several laptops and a solitary cup of tea before her, Dylan Dennis—rumored to not be her real name—was in her early seventies. Gray and gaunt with black horn-rimmed glasses and constantly in comfy, unremarkable attire, Dylan never attempted to better her appearance. Some believed it was a deliberate play at not drawing attention to herself, selling the whole used-bookstore-owner façade should nosy noses come sniffing.

But much like Einstein was rumored to have worn the same suit every day so as not to waste precious thought on something as insignificant as clothing, Caleb believed Dylan was in company with the likes of Einstein—time spent on appearance would mean time away from getting her thumbs in those pies, her ears next to valuable lips.

"I'm pleased to see you," Dylan went on. "Other than your memorable dining experience at Applebee's, I'd heard you got into quite another sticky little situation not long ago. Took out how many guns that were after your head?"

"Three," Caleb said.

"I was told five took the contract. And yet I hear Mia and Sampson Wykowski are still breathing."

"I had a moment of weakness." Truth was, Mia and Sampson Wykowski, a brother and sister team as ruthless and efficient as they came, had been uncharacteristically instrumental in Caleb's survival when a contract on Caleb's head had been offered last year. He owed them big-time, but was in no hurry to pay them back anytime soon. Unlike Caleb, who was a rarity in his vocation for only going after those who warranted going after, Mia and Sampson were as discriminating with job offers as sailors were to women after being out to sea for a spell.

Dylan laughed. "You are anything but weak, young man. To what do I owe the pleasure?"

"You mean you haven't heard?"

Dylan accepted Caleb's playful dig with another laugh. "Nice to see your wit was not damaged in that contract ordeal."

"It was probably the only thing that wasn't damaged." This was no lie. While Caleb had emerged from the contract ordeal still breathing, he'd suffered quite a few lumps along the way, some of those lumps popping in to say hello after the occasional sneeze or during a tough workout.

Another cat—an orange tabby—weaved its way through Caleb's shins. He looked down. "Who's this?"

"Agatha," Dylan replied. "She's in here with me because she

hasn't been feeling too well as of late. Some kind of intestinal thing."

As if on cue, Agatha went to the litterbox in the corner and took quite possibly the smelliest dump Caleb had ever smelled in his life. He pinched his nose. "Jesus…"

Dylan smiled, rose from her seat, sifted the litterbox, put the contents in a baggy, tossed them in a small receptacle next to the litter box, then broke out the deodorizer. She misted the room heavily with the stuff. Caleb wasn't sure what stunk worse, the cat poop or the deodorizer. The label on the can had read "ocean breeze," only it was anything but.

Satisfied, Dylan took her seat at the table again. "Poor thing," she said, glancing over at Agatha. "Might have to change her diet."

Brands of deodorizer too, Caleb thought.

"Speaking of cats," Caleb said, "anytime you want to part with Harper, I'll gladly take her off your hands."

"I thought you were a dog person."

"I'm an animal person."

"Well, I'm sorry—Harper's going nowhere."

"Figured as much."

"Okay, we got the banter out of the way," Dylan said. "You're here because…?"

"Actually, you *have* heard in a roundabout way. It's about the Applebee's thing. I need what I always need from you."

Dylan told the clerk to leave. He did.

"Go on," Dylan said.

Caleb relayed recent events.

"'Alexander,' he called himself?"

Caleb nodded. "Could have easily been a bullshit name, though."

Dylan removed her horn rims. "Can't say it's ringing any immediate bells."

"Any bells at all?"

"Some. You say he gave you no inclination whatsoever as to who his employers were?"

"None. Just talked a big game. But he did find me. And quickly. Even *my* team would have been jealous. Who else would have such resources?"

"Huh," she said.

"Huh what?"

Dylan muttered something to herself and then began to clack away on one of her laptops. Finished, she turned the laptop around so that its screen faced Caleb.

There he was. A candid photo of Alexander standing outside of a café with another man Caleb didn't recognize.

"Holy shit, that's him."

"Oh," was all Dylan said. But it was enough.

"What? 'Oh' what? Who are they?"

"I would do the job, Caleb. Just do it and get it over with."

"*Why?* Dylan, for the love of—"

"You've heard of blue eyes?" Dylan interrupted. "Well, these guys are Frankie Fucking Sinatra."

20

Blue eyes. It was a common term in the criminal underworld for police involvement. Rare, but it happened.

"What do you mean 'Frank Sinatra'?" Caleb asked.

"Their entire organization has blue eyes," Dylan said.

"Bullshit. They struck me as anything *but* cops. Alexander especially."

"They dress and act the part of wiseguys or whatever to divert attention away from who they really are."

"That's how they found me so quickly."

"Correct."

"It's why the three guys I knocked out in Applebee's didn't say anything to the police."

"They *were* the police."

Caleb thought about that. He wondered whether those three guys were still sleeping when (more) police showed. If so, did the police that showed on the scene recognize the three, or were they from different departments? The Applebee's was in Bucks County, in the 'burbs. The police that showed were likely a small department. Who were the guys *he* knocked out? What department were *they* with? This begged the question...

"How many?" Caleb asked.

"How many what?"

"How many blue eyes are we talking here?"

"No one really knows. But apparently it's substantial enough for concern among those in the city who try to cross them."

"The city. So it's Philly PD then?" Caleb asked.

"Again, no one really knows. To the best of my knowledge, it stretches further. They have hierarchy, though, just like organized crime. The guys you beat up *were* probably low-level. I know that Alexander has some status, though."

"So he claimed. He also claimed there were people above him. 'Rungs,' he called them."

"I'm sure there are." Dylan sipped more tea.

"So, what are we talking here, a corrupt department? Several corrupt departments working together?"

"Again, I don't know."

"I thought you were the person who knew shit."

"I *do* know shit; I'm telling you that shit now. All anyone knows is that there are more than a mere handful of dirty cops involved. It could be one department in the city, or could be several in the city and beyond. The guys you beat up were in a freaking Applebee's in the 'burbs, for God's sake. It could stretch that far, for all I know."

A freaking Applebee's in the 'burbs. He'd said almost the exact same thing to his team earlier.

This made Caleb revisit his earlier thoughts about whether or not the police that showed on the scene at the Applebee's had recognized the three he slept. Surely, if they did, news would have broke that the three men involved in the Applebee's affair were police officers... assuming the police that showed knew the three and were good cops.

Good cops.

Caleb liked the police. Had the greatest admiration for the dangerous job they did, day in and day out, and for what some might consider shitty pay, no less. He really didn't want to believe that the numbers in this "organization" were many and far.

Of course there was also the very real possibility that the three cops he'd knocked out woke up (unlike in the movies, people in real life are seldom unconscious for conveniently long times after a good punch), and hightailed it out of there before the

(good? he really hoped good)

police had even arrived.

"I would do the job, Caleb," Dylan said again. "That many blue eyes? Knowing who you are and what you do? Their resources?"

"You know how I work," Caleb said.

"Yes, I know your moral code. But please reconsider what I just said. They really could make your life miserable. I'm sure you've made peace with losing your own life years ago, but…the lives of others?" Dylan needn't expound on those "others."

"I could go after *them*," Caleb said. And this was more a thought out loud than an actual threat. "A bad cop is no different than the myriad of ass hats I kill for a living. Some might say worse. They took an oath to protect us from those ass hats."

"Where would you even start?" Dylan asked. "If it was three or four bad apples, or hell, even ten, I'd say it might be worth considering—I know what you can do—but we simply have no idea how many we're dealing with here."

Caleb felt a sudden annoyance at Dylan's use of "we," as though a sort of camaraderie might lessen his resolve.

"I do this one job for them, who's to say they won't be coming back to me for future ones? If they've got me by the balls, as you're so subtly implying, then who's to say?"

Dylan clearly registered Caleb's annoyance. She sipped the last of her tea and merely splayed a hand. "I suppose no one can say. If

Alexander was truthful with his whole atonement thing, then we—"

(*fucking "we" again*)

"—can only hope that once you 'atone,' things will be square in their eyes. Look at it this way, Caleb: this job they're asking you to do—dropping in on a big drug deal—it's not like the parties involved are salt of the earth. They'd fit right in with your moral code."

Caleb grunted. *So* many questions. And unfortunately, it appeared as though Dylan's well had run dry.

He did have one other resource he could go to, though. How useful that resource would prove to be was anyone's guess, but it was worth a shot.

Caleb thanked Dylan and left her office. The smell of the deodorizer was on his clothes, and though he could not wait to get home and change, he could not help but stop and say goodbye to Harper on the east sill first.

He then headed back to his apartment to call his friend Sheriff Chip Parsons in Noodle, Indiana.

21

Noodle, Indiana—a running joke between Caleb and his team, and anyone else who was on a need-to-know basis in Caleb's world:

Yes, there was a town called Noodle…and Caleb fucking loved the place.

At first, Caleb had likened Noodle to something out of the Old West, the likes of which Doc Holliday or Wild Bill would have felt right at home in, chewing its dirt. And while the small town did initially appear as such—one main road; centuries-old mom-and-pop shops on either side of that road; even a saloon that didn't just have the moniker in its title, but damn sure looked the part inside and out—Noodle's guts revealed a different place entirely. The town was a hidden gem, its kindness and charm only exceeded by its lifelong history of nonviolence.

Until Caleb arrived, that is.

In his self-proclaimed cursed way, Caleb had brought hell to Noodle. When an open contract had been taken out on Caleb's life, quite a few professionals had followed him to Noodle in Caleb's attempt to flee until things settled.

The result? Doc Holliday and Wild Bill might have been jealous of the blood that was spilled during Caleb's stay. Dead deputies; dead proprietors; the once sleepy town gaining notoriety for all the wrong reasons after Caleb had left.

But if there was one good thing to come from Caleb's stay at Noodle—other than his life—it was the friendship he'd formed with its sheriff. A man by the name of Chip Parsons. Their bond had begun to gel with pleasantries over food and drinks, only to be solidified with perhaps the strongest way bonds were formed. War.

Sheriff Parsons, a former cop from Indianapolis who'd been injured in the line of duty and placed on medical leave, only to go stir crazy after his wife passed, thus seeking out the "safe" job as sheriff in Noodle thereafter, had assisted Caleb in dispatching a particularly nasty assassin: the Serbian that Caleb had mentioned to Alexander in Caleb's living room—the assassin who had tasted his own flesh in the form of pâté, courtesy of Chef Caleb.

Sheriff Parsons had not come away unscathed from the ordeal, though. His ring and pinky finger had been cut off at the hands of the Serbian, in addition to a knife in the guts for his troubles.

Fingers since reattached, and knife wound to the gut healed, Caleb and Sheriff Parsons kept in touch whenever possible via phone calls and FaceTime. Today, Caleb wanted FaceTime.

A FEW RINGS, and then Parsons's face took up the bulk of the two images on Caleb's smartphone, Caleb's face small in the lower right corner. Caleb hated the small square in the lower right corner. Always felt it made him look as though he had a double chin.

"Why is it I still get nervous every time you call?" Parsons answered with a smile.

Caleb smiled back. It was good to see his friend. Plus he never got tired of Parsons's uncanny resemblance to the actor Ving Rhames, right down to the deep voice and bald head. But there was a new addition to Parsons's appearance this time around. A thin goatee.

Caleb gestured to his own mouth and said: "You've got something on your face."

Parsons stroked his facial hair and said: "Yeah, well you keep saying I remind you of Ving Rhames, so I'm trying for an Idris Elba look. What do you think?"

"I think you'll need a lot more than a goatee to look like Idris Elba."

"Ouch."

Caleb laughed. "How are the fingers?"

Parsons held up the middle one.

Caleb laughed again. "Dick."

Parsons grinned and then showed and flexed the ring and pinky fingers that had been reattached some time ago. "Stiff when it rains, but nearly good as new."

"Still wearing your wedding band, I see," Caleb said.

Parsons dropped his head and shook it. Not because it was a painful subject—his wife's passing—but because of the inside joke between the two of them as to how Caleb had recovered the ring for his friend during the debacle in Noodle. After slicing off Parsons's ring finger, the Serbian had swallowed the discarded wedding band in an act of pure malevolence. Once the Serbian was dead, Caleb took it upon himself to…"retrieve" the ring for Parsons. Enough said.

"You're a sick man," Parsons said after lifting his head.

"Which is why you still get nervous every time I call," Caleb said.

"Very true."

"And today you have every right to be," Caleb added.

Parsons's smile left. "Uh-oh."

"Yeah."

22

Caleb explained everything.

"And your source says she has no idea how many?" Parsons asked.

"Correct. Rumor is it's multiple departments fanning out from Philadelphia, working together."

Parsons made a face. "That's tough to swallow. Crooked cops here and there? Sure, it happens. But entire departments working together like some kind of criminal syndicate? Sounds a bit too much like fiction to me. In all my years in Indianapolis, I never heard of such a thing."

"They found me quickly, so they've definitely got some metaphorical muscle. Whether that means there's ten or a hundred, who knows. What's your gut telling you?"

"My gut tells me there's a few districts in your neck of the woods that don't know they have some assholes among them."

Now Caleb made a face. "Meaning what?"

"Let's say you've got district A that has a hundred cops. My guess is that maybe two or three in that district are dirty.

Somehow, those dirty cops from district A hooked up with a few dirty cops from district B. And so on and so on. Follow me? No way is an entire district, never mind a department, all working together."

"So, that brings us back to how many assholes from how many districts in those departments are working together," Caleb said.

"Yep."

"So, do you think you can do some digging for me?"

"What about your team? You said they were the best."

"They are, but I don't want them involved on this one. Will you do it for me?"

"I can certainly try. Might take some time, though. And it sounds like you don't *have* much time."

"I don't. My twenty-four hours is dwindling."

"So then, at the risk of being blunt, why do you want me to dig? *If* I find something, it will almost surely take more than twenty-four hours."

"Because something tells me that once I do this job for them, that won't be the end of it."

"You don't think they'll honor this 'atonement' thing? Call it even?"

"That's what they said, but I tend to think I'm still alive for refusing to believe what assholes say. I'm thinking there's a strong chance they'll try to threaten my friends and family to do more jobs like they did for this one, or that they'll try to off me once the job is done to tie up loose ends."

Parsons grunted his understanding. Then: "You want me to send some help?"

"Thanks, but I don't need any more dead deputies on my conscience."

Parsons shook his head. "No, no—these are different animals altogether. Retired cops who are now into private security. Tough as they come."

"Can you get 'em here in the next few hours?"

Parsons started to nod, conceding to Caleb's point. "Probably not."

"Then let's stick a pin in that for now. But after this is over, and my hunch about them wanting to tie up loose ends comes true, then I may just take you up on that offer. Question is, would *they* be up for it? Isn't there a brotherhood or code amongst you guys?"

"Oh, there's a brotherhood. But once you cross that line and become the very scum you used to risk your ass chasing night in and night out, you're on your own."

"I guess I'll have to take your word on that," Caleb said.

"After what we've been through together, I'd think my word would be enough."

"Don't get sensitive. Like I said, I tend to think I'm still alive by not believing what assholes have to say."

"Oh, so I'm an asshole now?"

Caleb laughed. "*So* sensitive."

Now Parsons laughed.

"How's Noodle?" Caleb asked.

Parsons broke eye contact. "It's fine."

"Just fine? I know it got a little crazy there after my delightful little visit, but you said things have died down since, yeah?"

Parsons still wouldn't make eye contact. He looked uneasy. "Yeah, it's all good."

"You know this is a FaceTime chat and not a phone call, right? I can fucking *see* you, man. What's going on?"

Parsons finally looked at Caleb. "You've got enough shit on your plate for now. We'll talk about it another time."

"Fine. But this is a to-be-continued chat."

"Just make sure *you* continue," Parsons said. "I'm still not wild about you going through with this."

"Trust me, I've weighed the options; I don't see many

alternatives. Best-case scenario is I take out some dickheads for some other dickheads and that's that."

"And the worst-case scenario?"

Caleb winked at Parsons. "To be continued."

Parsons went to say something, but Caleb hung up.

23

The clock was ticking. Caleb had roughly three hours before he was to meet with Alexander and a few others to get the specifics of what needed to be done. Location, primarily—best available entry and exit points, et cetera. He didn't like relying on anyone but his team for such crucial elements of a job, but his hands were tied on this one; Caleb was still as adamant as ever about keeping his team out of it.

The meeting spot was a bar in Philly. Caleb was to go to the bar and ask the bartender for a cosmopolitan. Apparently, it was the kind of bar where a guy did not typically order a cosmopolitan. After that, Caleb was told, the bartender would handle the rest, whatever the hell that meant.

That just left Rosco. When Caleb had left for Noodle, he had begged Dr. Flynn to look after him while he was gone, and to take care of Rosco if something were to happen to him in Noodle. Dr. Flynn had reluctantly agreed.

He wasn't so sure she'd agree to it this time.

CALEB WAS RIGHT.

"No," Dr. Flynn said before Caleb could even get a word out.

Caleb stood outside Dr. Flynn's front door with Rosco by his side. "No, what? I haven't said anything."

"No," Dr. Flynn said again.

"Please—this is the last time, I swear," Caleb said. "Consider it an act of charity for bumping me down to blowjobs."

Caleb's try at levity failed miserably; Dr. Flynn looked more annoyed than ever.

"Put him in a kennel," she said.

"Too late for that now. And who knows what the kennel would do with him if I couldn't come back to get him?"

"Caleb, I am your doctor. I crossed serious ethical boundaries the last time I took your dog."

Caleb could not help but laugh. "Ethical boundaries? Have you been awake for any of our sessions?"

"Barely."

Ah! She couldn't help herself on that one. I see a window.

"This won't be like last time. I'll collect him in less than forty-eight hours. Please—I'm begging you."

Dr. Flynn looked out onto the street. When she brought her attention back on Caleb, she said: "I have a condition."

"Anything."

"Weaning," was all she said.

"What about it? I already agreed to try."

"Give me your word you'll try harder. No more physical contact whatsoever."

Fuck. He hadn't expected that. Caleb looked down at Rosco. Rosco looked up at him, little tail flapping away. His love for the dog burned.

"Deal," Caleb said to her.

"I'm serious, Caleb. How important is me doing this for you?"

"Extremely."

"Well, as your doctor—as *anyone's* doctor—the patient's progress is extremely important to me as well. If you recall, I mentioned this to you when I first insisted on weaning: no competent therapist strives for routine with their patients. I'm no different."

An odd chink in the armor of Dr. Flynn? Her potent need for progress with patients? No, that was absurd. If anything, it was to be admired. Unless it was for her own satisfaction as opposed to the patient's.

Only Caleb didn't believe that, and he chastised himself for even thinking there might be a chink in her armor to exploit. Stoic as she was the majority of the time, Dr. Flynn cared about her patients' advancement, not her own. One of Caleb's greatest strengths was his ability to read people, and while Dr. Flynn was akin to *Moby Dick* in Spanish, he could still read a sense of virtue about her when it came to the job and mankind itself.

"I get it," Caleb said.

"If you go back on your word, Caleb, I will end our relationship immediately."

"How can I go back on my word if you won't allow it? I'm a lot of things, but I'm not the type to force myself on someone."

"I know you're not, but it doesn't mean you wouldn't try to convince me to change my mind. *That* I can see you doing."

This was unfortunately true. It was why he'd just chastised himself for looking for a chink in her armor to exploit. His horrible urges often had the habit of hijacking his tongue during their sessions when he wanted more than she was willing to give. God, how he hated himself for it.

Caleb then flashed on his drive home that day after their session when she'd first weaned him with the blowjob, the reflections he'd had, how the blowjob had actually done the job and done it well. How he was tired of being weak, addicted to his compulsion and all the hollow justifications that preceded that compulsion. How it made him feel that much weaker when the act was done.

How he wanted to get better.

And then there was Rosco. What better incentive did he need? It was stronger than his want to get better, though the two were hardly mutually exclusive. He could have both. He *would* have both.

"You have my word," Caleb said.

Dr. Flynn took Rosco's leash. Caleb bent and gave Rosco love.

"Forty-eight hours?" Dr. Flynn said.

Caleb stood. "Forty-eight hours."

Dr. Flynn said nothing more and went inside with Rosco, closing the door behind them.

Caleb swallowed his sorrow once Rosco was gone. Total and absolute resolve took over a second later. "I *will* have both," he now said aloud.

Drug dealers and crooked cops, no matter how many—someone was getting fucked up.

24

Caleb found the bar in Philly with little trouble. Its exterior was not flattering. Nor was the interior.

But was that really all so surprising? The bar's shoddy décor, both inside and out, was a likely deterrent to the majority. Business was conducted here, and it had nothing to do with pouring booze. Caleb would even wager that the odd patron who wandered in might perceive the same. Some places just had that "you lost, pal?" vibe.

Caleb took a stool at the bar. Save for him and the bartender, the place was empty. The bartender approached. He wore a dark green tracksuit. His thinning hair was slicked back. He was heavy. Caleb wondered whether he too was a cop.

"Cosmopolitan," Caleb said.

The bartender said nothing in return. Just turned his back to Caleb, picked up the receiver on an old-school landline, hit a single button on the keypad, said something that Caleb couldn't make out into the receiver, hung up, and then faced Caleb again.

"Out of Cointreau?" Caleb said.

The bartender gave Caleb a tough-guy face, and Caleb had to

bite back a laugh. How badly he'd like to reach over the bar and strangle the guy with the cord from that old-school phone.

Two men were soon at Caleb's side. Big men. Both in tracksuits of their own. Again, Caleb had to fight off a laugh. So desperate they were in trying to sell their whole wiseguy image. Still, he could not help but look their attire up and down, then at the bartender, then back at the two men at his side and say: "There a sale going on somewhere?"

"Get up and turn around," one of the two big men said.

Caleb did. He was patted down. The big man removed Caleb's Glock 17 from his waistband, a knife from his ankle holster, and his cell phone. The big man placed all three items on the bar. The bartender took them and tucked them away somewhere beneath the bar.

"You can have them back when you leave," the big man said.

"Why my phone?" Caleb asked.

The big man spun Caleb around by the shoulders and got in his face. The man's cologne was terrible yet somehow familiar. "Because I felt like it," the big man said.

The itch to headbutt the guy and splatter his face was like head-to-toe eczema. "Your world, boss," Caleb said.

"Let's go," the second of the two big men said.

"Go where?" Caleb asked.

Neither of the two replied, only turned and started towards a staircase at the end of the bar.

Caleb followed, still itchy.

25

Up the stairs and into what appeared to be the only room on the second floor of the bar. It was the total antithesis of downstairs. Various shades of smart red furnishings. Soft lighting. An oak bar to his right. A cushy lounge area to his left. Flat screen TVs on the walls. And directly ahead, at the far end of the room, behind the captain's wheel that was his vast cherrywood desk, sat Alexander, a big smile on his face, salt and pepper hair as neatly parted to one side as ever. Caleb began to wonder whether Alexander was full of shit, whether he was the top rung after all. He certainly acted the part.

Alexander splayed his hands, still smiling. "There he is."

"Here I am," Caleb said absently, not looking at Alexander, but taking inventory of the other occupants in the room instead.

There were seven in all, plus Alexander: the two big guys who'd led him upstairs, who now stood firm behind him like sentries; one behind the oak bar to his right, cutting lemons and limes; two on a large sofa to his left; and two by Alexander, each flanking the cherrywood desk.

Caleb, as was his way, without conscious effort, read each man from top to bottom.

And something wasn't right.

One of the men on the sofa—his pupils were dilated. He was either exceptionally aroused, or on something.

The man next to him on the sofa had tattoos up and down both forearms, and while tattoos were not typically frowned upon anymore within police departments, Caleb spotted a manacle tattooed on the man's left wrist, a common prison tattoo among Russians who'd served more than five years.

The man behind the bar cutting lemons and limes was doing a lousy job. He was doing it to appear unassuming as opposed to preparing them for cocktails.

The two men flanking Alexander were night and day. The one to Alexander's left was strong and composed; the one on his right, twitchy and weak.

And then there were the two men behind Caleb, the sentries. Caleb had read them downstairs and had found nothing out of the ordinary.

Conclusion? If there were cops in this room, there were only a few. The others were something else entirely, and while Caleb did not immediately dismiss the idea that this organization of corrupt cops could be affiliated with unsavory characters who never wore a badge, the air in the room told him something else was going on here.

"I wasn't impressive enough for you in my apartment?" Caleb asked Alexander.

Alexander cocked his head to one side. "Come again?"

"Suppose they kill me," Caleb said. "How will I be able to atone?"

Alexander smiled again. "You misunderstand; these men are here to accompany you on your job."

Caleb shook his head. "A—I work alone. B—bullshit."

CALEB: ATONEMENT

The man cutting lemons and limes attacked first. He rushed out from behind the bar and lunged at Caleb with the knife. He slashed twice, Caleb evading each, and then thrust the knife towards Caleb's throat. Caleb parried the stab, booted the guy in the nuts, picked up the knife the guy dropped while tending to his nuts, and then jammed the blade into the side of the man's neck, hitting the carotid, blood jetting in great spouts both before and after he hit the floor, dead.

The two men on the sofa attacked simultaneously. The Russian with the manacle tattoo drew a pistol. Caleb snatched a full bottle of vodka off the bar and threw it at him, catching him flush in the face, glass shattering, vodka, and blood spraying.

Manacle screamed and clutched his face, dropping the gun. The man with the dilated pupils dove for the discarded gun but met Caleb's foot instead. He was out cold from the first kick, but Caleb added a stomp "because he felt like it."

Caleb then quickly dropped to one knee, snatched up the pistol, put two bullets into the still screaming Manacle, two into unconscious Pupils, and then spun on his knee and aimed the gun at Alexander, but did not pull the trigger.

As Caleb had expected, the composed man to Alexander's left hadn't moved to enter the fray during the whole mess. Neither had the two big men who'd walked him upstairs. They did have their weapons drawn, however, and they of course were aimed at Caleb.

As for the twitchy one on Alexander's right? He too hadn't moved, but no weapon drawn from him. And if he'd looked twitchy before…

Still on one knee, Caleb kept the gun on Alexander. The spout of blood pumping from the neck of the man who'd been behind the bar was losing strength, reduced to a leak. Manacle and Pupils didn't move. That was a lie—Manacle's leg twitched from a death spasm.

Alexander showed Caleb his hands, yet appeared anything but concerned. "You look upset, Caleb."

"I'm guessing you wanted those men dead?" Caleb said.

"What makes you say that?"

"Because it was amateur hour. It wasn't a test at all, but you probably told them it was, didn't you? You wanted them dead because they betrayed you, outlived their use, or some other stupid shit—I don't really care—but I'm anything but upset. Actually, I'm quite happy."

"Spot on, Caleb. Once again, you continue to impress me. Though I do have to ask as to why you're happy?"

"Because I'm done," Caleb replied. "You wanted someone dead, I killed them, boom—we're done."

"I thought I made it clear as to who you were to kill for us," Alexander said.

"Oh, it was crystal," Caleb said, "but fuck you; you never said anything about this. In fact, you might have told me in advance without all the fucking drama of letting them 'test' me first. I could have offed them the second I walked in the door. Amateur or not, shit happens. Suppose the Russian got a shot off and killed me? Or even wounded me? How would I have done the job for you then?"

Alexander looked amused. "How did you know he was Russian?"

Caleb said nothing.

Alexander showed Caleb his hands again. "Okay, okay—perhaps I was given an inch and took a mile, or however the expression goes."

"Yeah, that's exactly what I was afraid of." Caleb stood and lowered his gun. He then raised his index finger. "One job. *One fucking job*. That was the deal."

Alexander motioned for the other men to lower their guns. They did.

"Again, I'm sorry for the theatrics, Caleb," Alexander began.

"The men you just killed *had* outlived their use to us. We also suspected they had stolen from us. However, some members of our organization were against getting rid of them—friendships and all that, if you will—only our hands were tied; the call was made from above. So, in order to make everyone happy, we decided to give the three men you killed a fighting chance by telling them we were testing you. I knew you'd have no trouble with them."

"Like I said, shit happens," Caleb said. "If one of them got lucky, not only would these three still be alive, but you wouldn't have me to disrupt your rival organization's drug deal, would you, genius?"

"But it didn't happen." Alexander smiled again.

Caleb shook his head. "You guys make me laugh. You act the part of wiseguys, but you're anything but. The mere fact that you were willing to give men who stole from you a fighting chance because it might hurt the feelings of a few other members of your crew is fucking pathetic. If your higher-ups had any balls, they'd have never hesitated to kill these three in their sleep."

Alexander's smile dissolved. "The 'higher-ups,' as you call them, don't know about what went on here. The execution of these three *was* supposed to come from within."

"Oh, so you took it upon yourself to do this? Your hierarchy sounds about as sturdy as a eunuch's cock."

"Are you finished?" Alexander said.

"Oh yeah—I already told you I was. Have a nice day, dickheads." Caleb turned towards the door. The two sentries got in his way. "If you guys want to end up like those three on the floor, then by all means make your move," Caleb said.

"Caleb," Alexander said behind him. "You know who we are; it's certainly no secret anymore. And I assure you, as competent as you are, we can and will make your life miserable for as long as we allow you to live it. Imagine having to adopt a new dog every week."

Caleb turned and faced Alexander.

Shoot him. Shoot them all. Kill them all. Deal with the rest later. Do it do it do it do it do it...

"You know," Caleb said, "your 'give a man an inch' expression makes me think of another."

"And that is?"

"Give a man enough rope and he'll hang himself."

"Meaning what exactly?"

"It'll make sense when it happens."

Alexander sighed. Again he asked: "Are you finished?"

Caleb said nothing.

Alexander gestured towards the twitchy man to his right. "Allow me to introduce your liaison for this evening..."

26

After Caleb had left the room, Alexander addressed the four who were still breathing.

"What did you think?"

One of the two sentries spoke. "I didn't like his attitude, what he was saying."

The second sentry: "Agreed. I question how trustworthy he is."

"He showed up, didn't he?" Alexander said. "As for what he was saying, he was just pissed off about getting attacked like he was. I'd be pissed off too, wouldn't you?"

All four men said nothing. A silent agreement.

"What did you think of his abilities?" Alexander asked.

The man to Alexander's left said: "Okay, I guess." His ego obviously had trouble giving Caleb credit.

Alexander looked up at the man to his left. "I see. So you would have been able to do the same? Unarmed?"

The man to his left sucked his teeth.

One of the sentries: "We already knew he was tough. I'm still not sure he can be trusted."

"He's tough *and* smart. Still not sure how he spotted Aleksei as

Russian," Alexander replied. "And then there was him clocking Marcus for who he was—" Alexander threw a thumb towards his right, where the twitchy man, Marcus, stood.

"Which is all the more worrisome," the sentry replied. "He might get ideas after he does the job."

"He'd be a fool to try anything," Alexander said. "He's smart enough to know that. Besides, it'll be irrelevant." Alexander picked up the receiver of the phone on his desk—another old-school landline—and dialed.

All four men listened intently.

"Yes, he showed," Alexander said into the receiver. "Yes, he left a few minutes ago to collect what he needed for the job…no, I don't suspect any; he'll do as he's told…yes, we'll take care of it once it's done…yes, we're well aware of what he's capable of; we have no intentions of meeting him head-on…of course; the second it's done." Alexander hung up.

"All good?" the man to Alexander's left asked.

"All good," Alexander replied. "For now at least." He turned in his chair and looked up at the man on his left. "So, you think Caleb was just okay?"

The man shrugged, his gesture affirming his position.

"Well, you better change your tune and start giving him a bit more credit, because when the time comes, the slightest mistake…"

27

Before Caleb had left the room above the bar:
"Allow me to introduce your liaison for the evening," Alexander had said. "Marcus, this is Caleb Lambert, a professional killer, who, as you might have noticed, is quite good at what he does."

Marcus was a small man with a slight build. Dark hair and eyes. A big nose. Caleb had thought he actually *looked* like a rat before it was announced—he'd clocked Marcus as no threat and a possible rodent the moment he'd read him. In fact, Caleb was confident he'd had it all figured out before Alexander had even begun explaining.

Marcus had stepped forward and actually extended his hand. The man to Alexander's left rolled his eyes.

Caleb looked at Marcus's outstretched hand. "What do you want me to do with that?"

Marcus sheepishly withdrew his hand and stepped back to his spot on Alexander's right.

"You should be nicer, Caleb," Alexander had said. "Marcus here is your ticket to a far easier task."

Caleb had voiced his assumption: "He's a member of your rival organization," he'd said. "He wants a career change. Figured he'd see if you were hiring. You told him you were, but on certain conditions. So, he's going to lead me to where the drug deal is and get me in the back door without bother. Tell me if I'm getting warm."

Alexander had grinned. "On fire."

The man to Alexander's left snorted contempt.

"Just tell me all I need to know," Caleb had said. "Don't bore me."

"Yes—I recall at your apartment how you prefer brevity. Marcus's associates—"

"*Former* associates," Marcus had interrupted.

Alexander looked over at Marcus with raised eyebrows that were cautioning, not inquisitive.

Caleb had hoped one of the three standing in the room would give Marcus a slap. It would have been the one bright spot of his evening thus far.

No one did, nor was it necessary; Alexander's expression had been enough. Still, he'd added: "Until your job is done, you are not even a fucking intern with us, Marcus. Understood?"

Marcus dropped his head and nodded.

Slap him, slap him, slap him, slap him, Caleb had begged the universe.

Alexander turned back to Caleb. "Marcus's *current* associates are having dinner later this evening with a prospective buyer. The deal is going down there. According to Marcus, there should be five: three of Marcus's associates—including Marcus—and two of the prospective buyers."

"Restaurant?" Caleb had said.

"You were expecting an abandoned warehouse or such?"

Caleb shrugged. "Restaurant is a little in plain sight."

"It's been our experience that the most successful transactions are done in plain sight. 'Hiding in,' and all that."

Caleb grunted, hating himself for agreeing with the prick.

"Keeping in line with your beloved brevity: Marcus will excuse himself to the bathroom, let you in the back entrance of the restaurant; you will enter, eliminate the remaining four at the table by whatever means you deem most efficient, grab the product and the money, and then exit through the same door from which you entered. A car should be waiting for you and Marcus by then. The car will bring you back here. Curt enough to your liking?"

"What about witnesses? Staff?" Caleb had said. "I won't kill innocents."

"We're all aware of your moral compass. Though I tend to think it will be a non-issue—witnesses and staff will likely be too frightened to act. *If* there happens to be a vigilante in your midst, then I trust you can incapacitate without killing?"

Caleb nodded once.

"Good. Marcus will give you the address of the restaurant. You can plug it into your GPS after retrieving your phone downstairs. Questions?"

"Nope."

"Not one?"

"Nope."

Alexander eyed Caleb suspiciously. "Need I remind you that we—"

"Nope."

Alexander looked away and slowly nodded. A deep breath, a slow exhale, and then, turning back towards Caleb: "Well, it's seven o'clock now. Might I suggest you go and collect whatever you may need for the evening and then hurry back so as not to miss your reservation?" Alexander smiled, pleased with his wit.

Caleb turned and faced the two sentries by the door again. "You gonna let me leave this time?"

The two men parted.

Caleb handed Manacle's pistol to one of them and left.

"What do you think?" Alexander asked the four who were still breathing...

28

Caleb hurried back to his apartment, a good thirty-minute drive if he gunned it. The job did not sound overly complicated, assuming they weren't leaving out anything of note, which was entirely possible with these assholes after the "test" bullshit they'd pulled in the upstairs room of the bar.

What would he need to do the job quickly and efficiently without placing any innocents in harm's way? All jobs were different. Some required excessive gear, some required nothing more than a good knife.

For this job, Caleb felt the best course of action was a baseball cap, a surgical mask, and his Glock 17 TB with its five-inch suppressor. That was all.

———

THE RESTAURANT WAS AN UPSCALE ONE, roughly ten minutes east of the bar. Caleb parked on the street one block over and made the remainder of the way on foot. Dressed in black sweats and a gray hoodie, his surgical mask and plain black baseball cap in one hand, Caleb ducked into the alley behind the restaurant. His Glock was holstered under his hoodie.

The alley was dimly lit but aided by the lampposts on the street behind him. There was a long line of dumpsters, each presumably marking the back end of an establishment, and a part of him could not help but wonder whether the assholes were planning on tossing him into one of those dumpsters once the job was done.

He hoped they were. How he'd love an excuse to kill them.

You'd bring down one hell of a shit storm.

(Fuck that. What should I do, let them keep coming after me?)

Caleb grunted justification to himself as he arrived at the back door of The Green Lion Grille. Apparently, they were known for their steaks. Shame he'd have to scratch this place off his list after tonight. In Caleb's world, a good steak was right behind his family and Rosco as far as love was concerned.

He was deep into the alley, the lampposts from the street no longer providing him decent light. All he had now was the solitary bulb above the establishment's rear entrance. But this was a good thing. After all, the less light he had on him, the better. No-brainer there.

Now to wait for Marcus to show his weaselly face.

CALEB DIDN'T HAVE to wait long. Marcus appeared a few minutes after Caleb had arrived at the back door of the restaurant. Opening the door just enough, Marcus fittingly snaked his way outside, bent, and placed a coaster from the restaurant in the doorway so the door would not lock behind them, and approached Caleb. He knew better than to extend his hand this time.

"You ready?" he asked Caleb. Marcus was wearing a handsome black suit, taking *maybe* a point or two off his ugliness.

"Is it as you said?" Caleb asked.

Marcus nodded, twitchy as ever.

"Four of them? No more? Don't let me get any surprises once I'm inside."

"Four—just four."

"How crowded is the restaurant?"

"Not very. A few couples at tables. One couple at the bar. You won't miss who you're looking for; they're the only table of four. All men in dark suits."

"Money and gear with them?" Caleb said.

Marcus nodded. "Both in briefcases under the table."

"They made the deal yet?"

Marcus shook his head. "They're still eating dinner. Doesn't matter though, right?"

Caleb supposed it didn't. Still, he couldn't give Marcus the satisfaction of admitting he had a point.

"Okay," Caleb said. "I'll meet you out here immediately after. Shouldn't take long. Car on its way?"

"That's what they told me," Marcus replied.

Caleb placed a firm hand on the back of Marcus's neck and squeezed just enough to let him feel his strength. The little man looked up at the big man with nervous eyes, the way an unfortunate might look up at his bully before he was about to be belted.

"You don't sound very convincing to me, Marcus," Caleb said. "Convince me."

"I only know as much as you do, man; I swear. Far as I know, the car will be here."

"No last-minute changes to the plan I should be aware of? I didn't like that stunt they pulled at the bar."

"Not that I know—I mean *no*…no."

Caleb took his hand off Marcus's neck. "See you in a few then."

29

Caleb poked his head inside the back entrance of The Green Lion Grille, hoping to spot no staff wandering by or loitering. There was none.

He put on the surgical mask

(*ah, COVID, how I do not miss you*)

and baseball cap, pulling the cap down tight so the visor would shield a solid view of his eyes, and made his way inside.

Caleb hurried towards the front of the entrance and immediately spotted the four men at the table, all dressed in black suits similar to Marcus's. He pulled his Glock.

A woman to his right screamed. Caleb paid her no mind and put a bullet in each of the four men at the table to stifle any immediate response from them. Then an additional bullet in each, all head shots to make sure they were gone.

Now a man to his left: *"Jesus Christ!"*

Caleb turned his gun on the man. The man threw up his hands and looked away. Caleb then waved the gun over the rest of the patrons and staff, and they too looked away. Some dropped their heads. The screaming woman was now crying.

Caleb spotted the two briefcases under the table, tucked the Glock into his waistband, grabbed the cases, and bolted.

30

The moment Caleb was back in the alley, he got behind the dumpster and wheeled it in front of the back door to block any exits.

He then turned. The car was there, engine running, waiting.

There was a driver, two men in the back seat (Caleb recognized one of them from the bar—the man who'd been standing to Alexander's left), and no one in the passenger seat.

No sign of Marcus whatsoever.

Two men in the back seat.

Empty passenger seat.

No Marcus.

Uh-uh...no fucking way.

Caleb set down the briefcases and rapped his knuckles on the rear window. One of the two men—the one who'd been to Alexander's left in the room above the bar—rolled down the window.

"Get in," the man said.

"Here—" Caleb handed the man both briefcases.

As the man busied both hands with the cases, Caleb pulled his

Glock and shot him in the head. Shot the man next to him in the head. Then the driver in the back of the head. *Pop! pop! pop!* in all of three seconds.

Caleb then opened the driver's side door, found the latch, and popped the trunk. Hurried towards the trunk, opened it, and there was Marcus, dead.

"Yep," Caleb said, and slammed the lid shut again.

He then took off his mask and cap, tossed them in the driver's lap, and started off down the alley, towards his car one block over.

He was *not* planning on heading home.

31

Caleb entered the bar ten minutes later. It was still empty, save for the bartender. Caleb approached and ordered a cosmopolitan. The bartender could only stare back at him, dumbfounded.

Caleb used the remaining bullets in his Glock on the bartender before popping the magazine and inserting another.

He headed for the stairs in back.

THE DOOR to the room above the bar was unlocked. Much as his rage wanted to kick it down and enter, guns blazing, Caleb's experience had taught him better. Such an abrupt course of action would cause a knee-jerk response from whoever was inside.

Better to casually enter, let the gravity of the situation seep its way in, causing a delayed response, much like the situation downstairs with the bartender. So often the devil could stand before you, nonchalant in declaring his evil intentions (or ordering a cosmo), and the human brain, to no fault of its own, would stop and consciously process the incredulity of it all instead of taking immediate action.

So, Caleb took a page from the devil's playbook and entered as though entering his own front door.

Alexander was there, behind his desk. The two sentries were there, in the lounge area, watching one of the big screen TVs. No one else.

And, as expected, all three gaped upon Caleb's entry, processing… processing…

"Gentlemen," Caleb said, composed as he shot both sentries three times each, culminating each of those three shots, as he always did, with a headshot.

Delayed response over, Alexander fumbled with one of his desk drawers and produced a gun too late—Caleb shot him in the shoulder of the hand holding the gun, and the pistol dropped, Alexander crying out and clutching his shoulder with his other hand.

Caleb moved in, gun on Alexander's head.

"Good news or bad news first?" Caleb said.

Alexander didn't reply, just continued grimacing in pain, continued clutching his wounded shoulder.

"Good news is that the job is done," Caleb said. "The men at the restaurant are dead. Bad news is I'm not."

"You just fucked yourself," Alexander eventually said, still grimacing, still clutching his shoulder.

"You sound like my shrink," Caleb said. "Who's the top rung?"

"Fuck you."

Caleb shot him in the other shoulder. Alexander cried out again.

"Who's the top rung? Tell me who and where they are."

"You're dead. Your dog is dead. Your family is dead. Your whole fucking world is—"

Caleb reached over the desk, took hold of Alexander's scalp

with one hand, and jerked him out of his chair and onto the floor, Alexander's feet knocking this and that off his desk as they trailed behind.

Caleb placed a heavy foot on Alexander's chest, pinning him where he lay.

"Top rung—who and where?" Caleb said again.

Alexander spat up at him.

Caleb shot him in the kneecap. Alexander's knee scream dwarfed his shoulder screams.

Caleb had to keep from smiling, his dark side taking center stage, Alexander's screams like applause. "I'm in no hurry whatsoever, you pretentious little prick...never getting those manicured hands of yours dirty. In fact—" Caleb bent, took hold of two fingers on Alexander's right hand, and snapped them like twigs.

Another excruciating cry.

Caleb felt the familiar tingle he both loved and resented.

"Getting old yet?" Caleb asked. "According to you, I'm already in deep shit, so I've really got nothing to lose by keeping this up all night, do I?"

Alexander just continued to writhe in agony.

"Top ruuuung..." Caleb sang.

"Even if I told you, it wouldn't do any good," Alexander finally replied. "You'd stand no chance."

"I beg to differ—I'm an ace at games of chance. Just call the three douchebags you sent to pick me up at The Green Lion and ask them. Can't promise they'll answer, though. Actually, speaking of calling..." Caleb went to Alexander's desk. He didn't want the landline; he was looking for Alexander's cell. It was not on the desk, nor in the drawers that Caleb rifled through.

He returned to Alexander and started going through his pockets. Alexander didn't—couldn't—resist. Caleb found the phone in Alexander's front pocket and pulled it. While it was likely that much of their business was conducted on landlines to avoid easier eavesdropping, Caleb found it difficult to believe that at least some of that business wasn't conducted on cell phones, especially on the road.

"Gimme your code," Caleb said.

"Fuck you."

Caleb shot him in the foot. Alexander's cries were whimpers now.

"Code," Caleb said again.

Alexander gave it to him. Caleb punched it in, and Alexander's smartphone came to life. Satisfied, Caleb pocketed the phone; he would go through its contents later.

Back to Alexander. "I think we're almost done here," Caleb said. "Last chance to tell me who the top rung is. I *will* find out eventually, but if you tell me now, I'll kill you quick. If you don't, I'll shoot you in the dick first."

Alexander, despite his previous—and Caleb hated to admit, somewhat admirable, considering his pain—attempts at bravado, now looked up at Caleb with horrified eyes. Here was a man with more holes in his body than a screen door, yet the mere mention of adding another hole into his dick…

"Ogilvy," Alexander said.

"Who? Did you say Ogilvy?"

Alexander nodded.

"That his first name or last name?"

"Last."

"Give me the first."

"Sam."

"*Sam Ogilvy?* That's his full name?"

Alexander nodded again.

"And he's the top rung?"

"Chief of police…" Alexander said weakly. He appeared to be fading.

"Where? What department? What precinct? Is he here in Philly?"

"He's too protected…they'll eat you alive."

"I remember you saying how impressed you were with me," Caleb said. "Has that admiration left the room?"

"His protection is better than you."

"They cops? His protection? They cops too?"

Alexander said nothing.

"They cops too, or are they something else?" Cops, no matter how many, would never have the training Caleb had. But if they were something else…

Alexander remained quiet.

Caleb dug his Glock's suppressor into Alexander's groin. "They cops, or something else? Three seconds: three…two…"

"*Something else! Something else!*" Alexander blurted.

"Like what? Something else like what?" Caleb said.

"I don't know," Alexander said. "Like you, maybe; I honestly don't know their background. On my mother's soul."

"Soul? Your mom dead?"

Alexander nodded.

"Did you love her?"

Alexander nodded again.

"Remember in my apartment when you asked me if I was a religious man?"

Nod.

"Are *you*?"

Nod.

"So, you believe in the afterlife?"

Nod.

"Well, then, you're welcome." Caleb shot Alexander between the eyes, reuniting him with his mother. Or perhaps he didn't—Caleb didn't know or care.

He left with Alexander's phone and the name Sam Ogilvy.

32

Sam Ogilvy—sixty-six, full head of white hair, blue eyes, lean—fixed himself a drink from his home bar. Asombroso Del Porto Extra Añejo tequila, neat. At fifteen hundred dollars a bottle, he was generous with the pour.

Behind him, in his lavish dining room, four well-dressed men sat at his dining room table, leaning into one another, speaking in hushed tones. Their muscle—three men, equally well-dressed, yet looking anything but dapper with their bulky frames stretching the lines of their suits—stood behind them, hands down and clasped together before their genitals in the fig leaf position: a conscious act to look secure, and a subconscious act to *feel* secure.

Scott Price—thirty-five, shaved head, black eyes matching his soul—approached Ogilvy.

"Sir," Price said. "I think they're close to accepting our terms."

Ogilvy sipped his tequila. "No they're not. They're stalling for time. Hoping we'll give in to theirs."

Price looked back at the dining room table.

"Give them a few more minutes," Ogilvy added. "If they don't come to a conclusion, remind them our offer is non-negotiable." It was a large but routine drug deal; old hat to Ogilvy.

Tony Decker—thirty-four, his head also shaved, his moral compass equally as black as Price's—approached now. He'd noticed Ogilvy and Price's little exchange.

"What's up?" Decker asked.

"Boss says thinks they're stalling for time," Price said. "Says to give them a few minutes, then to remind them they're fucked if they don't accept."

Now it was Decker who glanced back at the dining room table. Then back to Ogilvy: "And if they say 'no'?"

"Make them say 'yes,'" Ogilvy said.

Decker flicked his chin at Price. "What do you think?"

Price looked over at the table again. More specifically, the muscle standing behind the men at the table.

"Hands are over their junk. They're trying to look the part, but they're really just covering their junk. Means they feel vulnerable," Price said.

Decker grunted in agreement.

Price played with his earlobe, a habit when aroused by the prospect of violence.

Decker noticed his partner's unconscious gesture and smiled to himself. He often thought Halloween masks should be of Price.

Someone at the dining room table cleared his throat. Ogilvy looked. One of the suits—the head man—waved him over. Ogilvy looked annoyed with the "here, boy!" gesture, but downed the remainder of his tequila and went anyway. Decker and Price followed close behind.

"Gentlemen?" Ogilvy said, arriving at the table.

"We're going to need twenty percent to make it work," the head suit who'd waved him over said.

"Fifteen," Ogilvy said. "I'm afraid that offer is set in stone."

"Stone can be broken," the head suit said.

"So can skulls," Ogilvy said.

The muscle behind the suits fidgeted.

Price played with his earlobe.

The head suit smiled an unfriendly smile. "Your math is as poor as your intimidation, my friend. I count seven of us, and only three of you."

"Math can be all about perception, *my friend*," Ogilvy said. "For instance, if I were to draw a six on the table, my men and I would see a six. Your men, however, would see a nine."

"Meaning what exactly?"

"Meaning that in this particular situation, three is far greater than seven."

The unfriendly smile again. "Is that a fact?"

"It is."

No one spoke. The muscle continued to fidget, hands still covering their groins. Price was close to removing his own earlobe. Decker was grinning.

"If you want to get physical here, then by all means make a move," Ogilvy said. "But I should point out that doing so will benefit no one, with the exception of my boys' blood lust, that is."

All fourteen eyes of the suits and muscle fell on Price and Decker. The suits appeared unfazed, confident. The muscle did not; much like a weaker animal senses it is in the room with an alpha without any tangible evidence to support the notion, so too was the muscle sensing the same now. Kittens to Price and Decker's lions.

"Twenty," the head suit said again.

"Fifteen," Ogilvy replied. "Final offer."

The head suit gave the unfriendly smile yet again, sighed, and began a slow nod. "You have the product here with you now?"

Now Ogilvy smiled, only his was genuine. Old hat, indeed. "Oh,

JEFF MENAPACE

I do love a good cliché," he said. He then cleared his throat, and with deliberate theatrics: *"Do you have the money?"*

The head suit played along. *"We do."*

"Well, then I guess you better get busy killing us and taking both the product *and* the money."

Muscle number one twitched.

Price need not have seen more. He leapt and drove all eight inches of his tactical knife into the eye socket of muscle one, spun and sliced the throat of muscle two, dropped low and drove the knife into both femoral arteries of muscle three's legs one after the other, then rose and greeted muscle three's dying scream with a grin.

The suits? Decker would have had a tougher time with a middle school football team.

Still, they made a try for it all the same, fumbling to pull their guns as Decker pounced, he too with a tactical knife. A thrust in the temple here, a couple of slashed carotids there, all leading up to the head suit who was saved for last as the grand recipient of a "Glasgow smile"—slicing a victim's mouth from ear to ear, creating an oversized grin. Typically, not a lethal assault...unless you were Decker.

Decker cut so deep that the man's head and mouth was like that of a hand-held puppet's, nearly in two.

Price played with his earlobe, Ogilvy went to the bar to refill his tequila glass, and Decker watched with great satisfaction as the head suit choked to death on his own blood.

Ogilvy returned with his drink. "Knives?" he said to his two men. "Hardly the quickest of methods."

"Funnest, though," Price said.

Ogilvy looked at the head suit's new smile, then at Decker. "That was excessive."

"I thought you'd appreciate the irony; the way he kept grinning at you like an asshole," Decker said.

Ogilvy held up a hand. "Oh, I'm not complaining."

Decker nodded, proud.

Ogilvy gestured towards the briefcase at the head suit's feet. "Go grab it, see if it really does have the money in it. If it doesn't, I want you to cut the rest of his fucking head off."

33

Back in his car, Caleb found a Burger King in a shady part of the city and parked in its lot. He had stopped to check Alexander's phone, but was also feeling that goddamn tingle he felt after such intense violence.

He thought about making Dr. Flynn proud by jerking off, but really wasn't keen on being spotted for such a display in a Burger King parking lot. So what else was there to do—of the immediate-need-for-gratification kind—when the primary need could not be fulfilled?

Caleb pulled into the drive-through, ordered a bacon double cheeseburger, parked in the lot again, and housed the burger in five bites.

CALEB'S STOMACH was burbling regret. The burger had, to no surprise, proved to be a lousy substitute for sexual release, but it was something. And dare he say there was a silly parallel? How many men and women had regret after that one-night stand? How many had regret after eating junk that made your colon cry? Sex and junk food. Go figure.

Shut up and check the phone.

Caleb started to do just that when someone rapped on his driver's side window. It was a young man in a hoodie. He appeared strung out.

Caleb did not roll down the window. "*What?*" he said through the glass. He was not friendly about it.

"Can you help me out?" the man asked.

"With what?"

"I gotta get home. I need a few bucks for the bus."

Sure you do.

"Sorry—can't help you," Caleb said.

The man tapped a pistol on the window. Caleb sighed and rolled down the window.

"Out of the car," the man said, putting the gun to Caleb's head.

Caleb went as though going to open the door, but grabbed the man's wrist instead, jerking him forward, the man's head colliding with the roof's steel edge, knocking him cold, the gun coming free and landing on Caleb's lap.

Caleb popped the magazine on the pistol, pulled the slide back to expel the remaining bullet in the chamber, and then tossed the empty gun out the window.

Caleb could hear the man moaning on the ground as he was coming to. He exited the car, stomped on the man's face, sending him back to bed, and then re-entered his vehicle. His heart rate was surprisingly even during the whole episode. But then why wouldn't it be? Candy from a baby had never been more fitting.

Back to work.

Caleb punched in Alexander's code and went through the list of recent calls, hoping, but not expecting, that one of the numbers might jump out at him. His endgame was to forward the numbers to Parsons and have him run them to see what he might find. He had the name Sam Ogilvy, and that was good, but finding him was another matter entirely.

Only it never got to that. Because the unexpected *did* happen.

Caleb recognized one of the numbers.

In fact, the number he recognized had been dialed and received quite a few times from Alexander's phone.

"*Motherfucker,*" Caleb mumbled to himself.

He then flashed on something he'd read about how powerful scent could be in triggering memory recall without conscious effort. Perhaps more powerful than any other sense when it came to memory. This revelation was a mixed bag for Caleb—good because it provided him one hell of a lead; bad because he was pissed off he hadn't processed it sooner.

It came to Caleb now like fragmented scenes in a film, the quality of the film excellent:

When Caleb had first visited the organization's bar.

When one of the two men had patted him down.

When Caleb had asked the man why he'd taken his phone in addition to his weapons, and the man had immediately gotten into Caleb's face. The terrible yet familiar stench of his cologne.

It wasn't cologne.

It was the same scent that had clung to Caleb's clothes after leaving Dylan's Den. The smell of the cat deodorizer Dylan had sprayed all over the place after her orange tabby Agatha had taken her titanic dump.

Dylan Dennis of Dylan's Den, renowned for an ear that stretched countrywide, had some fucking explaining to do.

Caleb intentionally ran over the unconscious man's feet on his way out of the lot.

34

For the second time this week, Caleb entered Dylan's Den. It was late, and the patrons were few. This was a good thing—Caleb had no idea what might end up happening. He certainly had no intentions of hurting Dylan, but if she had visitors…

No time for Harper on the east sill during this visit. Caleb made a beeline for the front desk. The same clerk as last time—small, thin, bad comb-over—was behind the desk.

"Can I help you?" Again, the man played the game, acting as though he didn't recognize Caleb, despite his very recent visit.

This only served to piss Caleb off that much further. He would not play the game back. No request for a rare book, no five hundred dollar bill, just: "I want to see Dylan."

"I'm sorry," the clerk said, "but she's very busy at the moment. If you'd like to leave your name—"

"*Stop*—you know who the fuck I am. Take me to her now, or I'll go myself and kick the fucking door down."

The clerk reached for the phone on his desk. Caleb caught his hand and squeezed with the intent to crush the man's bones. The clerk winced and looked as if he was preparing to shout. Caleb jerked him forward and slapped a hand over his mouth.

"Shhhh..." Caleb whispered. *"This is a bookstore; people are trying to read. Take me to her or I'll go myself* and *break your fucking hand."* He squeezed harder.

The clerk looked as though he might drop to his knees from the pain. He eventually nodded. Caleb let go.

"Run, shout, or do anything stupid, and I won't just stop at your hand," Caleb said.

The clerk led him towards the back of the store without further trouble.

35

The clerk opened the door to Dylan's office. Caleb shoved him inside and entered right after. Turned and shut the door.

Dylan was at her usual spot, alone at the head of the only table in the room, laptops and a cup of tea before her. Her comfy attire was as unremarkable as ever, horn rims as horny

(ha!)

as ever.

"Caleb," she said, eyes wide behind those horn rims. "What on earth?"

"I think you know," Caleb said. "Don't insult me by pretending you don't."

Dylan dropped her gaze on the table.

"You know, I should have known from the start," Caleb said. "When I asked you if I could have Harper, you said you thought I was a dog person. Why would you assume that? We get along well enough on the odd occasion that I need your services, but we're not friends; I never told you I'd recently gotten a dog. Someone else must have told you. Someone who'd recently been to my apartment and met him, fucking *threatened* him." Caleb felt his rage taunting his composure. It took effort to contain it.

Dylan looked up. "That's it? That's how you found out?"

"No. There was more." He glanced around the room but could not spot Agatha. He hoped her stomach issues hadn't resulted in something serious.

"Did you do the job?" Dylan asked.

"I'll get to that. Answer me this one question. Don't lie or I'll know. Is your real name Samantha? *Sam?*"

"What?"

"Answer."

"No, it's not. It really is Dylan."

She seemed to be telling the truth. "But you know why I asked you that, don't you?"

Dylan dropped her gaze on the table again.

"Sam Ogilvy," Caleb said. "He's the top rung. Chief of police too, I hear. Just not sure where. Alexander told me this just before I killed him."

Caleb expected Dylan's head to pop right up with shock, but instead she merely shook it and removed her horn rims. "Oh, Caleb, you didn't."

"I did. Call me impulsive, but I have this thing about killing people before they kill me."

Dylan sipped her tea. Her hand shook a little. "So, you did the job and then they tried to tie up loose ends."

"Correct. And something tells me you knew that would happen."

"I suspected it was a possibility."

"The way you kept pushing me to do the job, that it was the smart thing to do. Your whole song and dance about pretending not to know who Alexander was at first, who he was with…tell me why I shouldn't fucking kill you right now."

"I was trying to *help* you, Caleb. You were in a no-win situation. *I* happen to consider you a friend."

"*Help* me? By telling them who I was and what I was about? By sending them to my fucking apartment?!"

"Yes. I knew what they wanted from you. If you did the job, then there was a chance they might have called it square. Not the greatest of odds, but it was *something*, wasn't it?"

"What's your connection to them?"

The clerk cleared his throat. "I should probably get back out front in case someone needs—"

"You should probably shut the fuck up and stay put," Caleb said.

The clerk did.

"My connection to them is the same as it is to any other contact I deal with," Dylan said. "Only more often than not, they pay me with my life."

"And so visiting you in order to get my address so quickly, to find out who I was, that was a 'pay with your life' kind of thing?"

"Yes."

"And afterwards? There had to be two visits for you to know about my dog."

"There were. Alexander told me about the two men you killed in your apartment, that now you really owed them. He also suspected you might be coming to me for information about who they were after your request for twenty-four hours. He was right, of course, and again, I was paid with my life to play dumb, to try to persuade you to do the job. My mentioning your dog was just for-real dumb on my part."

"So, you're not affiliated with them in any official sort of way whatsoever? Just a scared contractor who does whatever they say in order to save your ass."

"Yes."

She still appeared to be telling the truth. She also appeared to be growing more unnerved by the minute.

JEFF MENAPACE

"Sam Ogilvy," Caleb said. "You know him? Or her?"

"Him. And yes, I do."

"Then do what you do best. Tell me where to find him."

"I'm dead if I do."

"You're *very* dead if you don't."

The office door opened. A big man stepped inside. He looked Caleb up and down. Glanced over at Dylan. "Is there a prob—?"

Caleb whipped a left hook into the man's jawline as though trying to crack cement. The man crumbled on the spot, sound asleep.

Caleb turned back towards Dylan and the clerk. Dylan looked frightened; the clerk, like he was about to shit himself.

"Now, why would he come in, you think?" Caleb asked them both.

Dylan showed Caleb her palms. "I have no idea."

Caleb looked at the clerk. He said nothing. He had something behind his back.

"Give it here," Caleb said.

The clerk handed over the cell phone.

"You texted for help behind your back?" Caleb said. "That's pretty impressive." He dropped the phone, stomped on it, then drove a right hand into the clerk's chin, literally launching him across the room and into an unconscious heap in the corner. He didn't want to hurt the little guy if he didn't have to, but was past caring now.

"This is getting messy, Dylan." Caleb pulled his Glock and aimed it at her face. "I have nothing to lose at this point. Tell me where to find Sam Ogilvy."

"He's heavily protected."

"So I've heard. Where is he?"

Dylan hesitated.

Caleb shot the sleeping big man twice in the chest.

Dylan slapped a hand to her mouth.

130

"Dylan, you know what I'm capable of, but I'm not sure you know just how fucking dark I can get." He aimed the gun at the clerk in the corner.

"*Don't*," Dylan said. "Please don't."

"How do I find Sam Ogilvy?"

"Take Harper," Dylan said. "She's yours."

"Much as I'd like to, I wouldn't dream of taking her from her sill." He approached the clerk and aimed his Glock down on him. "Tell me how to find Ogilvy now, or I'll kill him."

"*Fuck*," Dylan muttered.

"You said you told me to do the job because you were trying to help me," Caleb said. "That *you* considered me a friend. If you truly meant that, then help me now. When I find Ogilvy, I assure you I will kill him and every other asshole in his crew deader than dead. That'll be the end of it, and you'll be safe."

Dylan sipped the last of her tea, hand shakier than ever. "He's a sugar daddy."

"Come again?"

"He's a sugar daddy—he's got a few women set up across the city and surrounding 'burbs. They live like queens in exchange for…you know."

"How many queens?" Caleb asked.

"Three, I think."

"You think?"

"Three."

"Give me a picture of Ogilvy and the addresses of the queens and we're done here."

Dylan nodded.

"And that picture and those addresses better be legit," Caleb added. "And if you try to call when I leave, try and warn them I'm coming, I'll survive. I always do. And the first stop I'll make on my way back is here. I won't make it quick either, Dylan."

36

Caleb called Parsons the moment he was back in his car. Another FaceTime.

"I'm always a little nervous when you call, but looking at you now, I'm really nervous," Parsons said. He'd since shaven his goatee.

"Do I look that annoyed?"

"You do."

"Well, for good reason," Caleb replied. "Things went from bad, to worse, to vegan."

"Yikes."

"Yep. See you shaved that nonsense around your mouth."

Parsons rubbed his smooth face. "Going for the Denzel look now."

"Can you at least pick an actor who isn't ridiculously handsome? Your bar is like to the fucking moon."

"I hate you."

"Anything for me?" Caleb said.

"Can't say I've found anything useful. I'm still digging, though."

"No worries," Caleb said, "I might have all I need for now. Except one thing."

"Which is?"

"Those guys you mentioned. The retired cops who could help me out. You think they'd be up for it?"

"Already spoke to them. Told them the story. They're up for it and then some."

"How legit are they?"

"Legit?"

"How *trained* are they? No offense, but a cop's training is nothing like mine or some of the other professionals I know. Can they handle themselves? I mean *really* handle themselves against guys who know what they're doing?"

"Offense taken. However, both are decorated Marines in addition to being cops. One was a sniper with more confirmed kills than you have issues."

"That's a lot of kills."

"They're as well-trained and seasoned as they come. But wait, hold on a second here—what are you worried about elite training for? Aren't you just going up against us lowly cops?"

"Apparently, the head guy has protection that's top shelf."

"Ah."

"So, your guys," Caleb said again, "they're definitely legit?"

Parsons nodded.

"Would you trust them to have your back?"

"A hundred percent."

"Okay. I'm gonna hang up and text you a bunch of shit, including numbers from a cell I want you to run, just in case. I'll be giving you an address on where your guys can find me. How soon *would* they be able to find me, you think? Money is no object."

"Don't worry about money for now," Parsons said. "And if I told them to punch it, they'd be there as soon as possible."

"Okay, good. And don't think I forgot about your lame attempt at telling me things were fine in Noodle."

Parsons broke eye contact. "Things are fine."

"I can fucking *see* you."

Parsons made eye contact again. "Can we just focus on you for now?"

"Fine. I'll text you what you need. Tell your boys it might get messy."

"They'll like that."

"They shouldn't. To be continued."

Parsons started to repeat the lines of their recent exchange that included "*you* continue," but Caleb hung up on him, just like last time.

Despite the fact that he might die in the next few days, doing that made him smile.

37

So many damned clocks ticking lately. The twenty-four hours Alexander had initially given Caleb to "consider" his offer. The forty-eight hours Dr. Flynn had given Caleb to return and collect Rosco. The who-knew-how-many hours before Ogilvy discovered what Caleb had done.

People needed to die, and quickly.

It was nearly midnight, and it was only a matter of time before Ogilvy and whoever the hell else had his back would hear about the colossal mess Caleb had left in both the alley of The Green Lion Grille, and in the bar. Not the least of that mess being Alexander himself, who Caleb was beginning to surmise, was Ogilvy's number two.

So, what would that make Alexander? If Ogilvy was chief of police somewhere, what was below chief of police? In a legit department, it could be anything from captain, lieutenant, sergeant…

Only this was anything but a legit department. Who knew how the hierarchy of their stupid organization worked? Bunch of crooked cops acting the part of wiseguys—for all Caleb knew, Ogilvy was the "boss," and Alexander was the "underboss," or the "consigliere," or however the hell it worked,

(mental note: watch more mob films when this is over)

but one thing Caleb *did* know was that whatever rank Alexander held in the organization, he had his cell phone.

And Ogilvy had yet to call.

Strange. Surely he'd have called by now to check the status of what had gone down this evening. If Dylan had been telling the truth—and Caleb still believed she had been—then perhaps Ogilvy was busying himself with one of his queens. Business was business, but sex was sex, the latter of which was undefeated when it came to priorities in men.

Caleb silently thanked the penis, and checked his watch again. Parsons had told him his men should be there shortly after midnight, "there" being a vacant lot in a town roughly fifteen miles outside of the city. Not the prettiest of towns. The street lamps that worked were weak or flickering; the few cars visible beneath those streetlamps, either stripped or long-since abandoned. Plenty of graffiti, some of it amusing, but most gang-related. A battered water tower in the distance, it too sporting gang-related graffiti.

Determined gang member, Caleb thought. *It was quite the climb.*

Caleb checked his watch again. It was now past midnight. Tick tock, tick tock. To say Caleb was anxious to get the ball rolling was not worth saying. And of course he had to piss. Risk doing it in one of the darker corners of the lot? Be a hell of a way to meet Parsons's men. Have them roll up on him while he was urinating in public? Not the best of first appearances.

Screw it; his bladder didn't care. Better to do it now and get it over with, instead of a quick "nice to meet you, fellas. Parsons told me good things. Now hold on a sec while I take a leak, if you don't mind."

Caleb hurried over towards one of those dark corners of the lot, unzipped, started to pee, and then heard the unmistakable click of a pistol's hammer being cocked behind him.

One of the many artists responsible for the gang-related graffiti perhaps? No, he would have spotted them coming a mile away. Caleb knew who it was, and he smiled inside. Parsons wasn't kidding; his guys were good.

"Thought you were elite," the voice behind him said. It was a gravelly voice, one likely tarnished from years of cigarette abuse. Caleb hoped the man's cardio wasn't lacking.

Caleb kept right on pissing when he replied: "Mind if I finish before you shoot? It stings when you pinch it off."

"You know I'm not gonna shoot, but I'd be lying if I said I wasn't a little disappointed."

Caleb finished, zipped up, and then slowly turned. The man before him matched his voice. Rough and gravelly. He had gray hair and a beard, also gray. He kept his six-shooter

(*of course the old fella has a six-shooter*, Caleb thought, smiling to himself again. *Colt Python .357, a legendary—and damned good—gun*)

on Caleb.

"Sorry to disappoint," Caleb said. "You are?"

"Jackson," the man said.

"First name or last?"

"Both."

"Jackson Jackson? Three more and we'd have...come on, you know where I'm going with this." Caleb started singing "ABC" by the Jackson 5.

"Too bad your awareness isn't as good as your humor," Jackson said.

"Sorry. Default for when I'm nervous."

"Lacking awareness *and* nervous? Maybe I've got the wrong guy."

"No, you've got the right guy. Caleb. Pleased to meet you,

Jackson." Caleb held out his right hand, the one he'd just pissed with.

Jackson looked down at Caleb's hand and made a face.

It was all the distraction Caleb needed. A blink, and Caleb had disarmed Jackson, the man's Colt Python now in his right hand, pressed tight to Jackson's temple, his left arm around Jackson's neck as though he meant to use him as a human shield.

And he meant to, or at least give the impression he meant to.

"*Motherfucker*," Jackson said behind gritted teeth, behind Caleb's forearm.

"Winning you over yet?" Caleb asked.

"Hardly," Jackson said.

"Why, because of your boy in the water tower?" Caleb asked. "I was told one of you was a sniper. Water tower would be the best place. He got a bead on me?" Caleb looked up towards the water tower. "*Think you can get me without getting him?!*" he yelled towards the tower, then shifted his grip from a left arm around Jackson's throat, to a firm hand around the back of his collar, squatting behind him, Colt Python now pressed into Jackson's back.

"In his sleep," Jackson replied for the mystery man in the water tower.

"Yeah?" Caleb said. "He that good?"

"Wait and see," Jackson said.

Caleb smiled inside for what seemed like the umpteenth time tonight. "Well, then let's make it interesting." Still gripping Jackson's collar from behind, Caleb set the Colt Python to the ground, went into his pocket, pulled a small remote device, and hit the solitary button on it.

Even in the distant night, the sudden cloud of smoke, initiated by a pop and a hiss, engulfed the top of the water tower completely.

"Oh shit," Jackson said.

"Yep," Caleb said. He pocketed the remote and picked the six-shooter back up. "This is the part when I tell you that could have been a bomb, and that I could now shoot you with your own gun, if I wanted."

"Assuming I didn't shoot you first when your dumb ass was taking a piss."

"Unless I knew you were there and was taking a piss on purpose to lower your guard."

This was a lie. Caleb suspected the dick-measuring might extend to the sniper climbing the clock tower for some fun and games, hence the smoke bomb, but he really did have to take a wicked leak—Jackson got him fair and square on that one.

Jackson called him on it. "Bullshit—you were going like a fucking camel."

"How's the view from up there?!" Caleb called towards the tower. *"Still think you can get me without getting—"*

POP!

A circle of red splattered against Caleb's left shoulder. It stung like hell and Caleb said, *"Ow, fuck!"* before letting go of Jackson, taking a few steps back and then—

POP! number two, a circle of red right over his heart—a kill shot.

If the shot had been intended to kill.

If the shot had carried a bullet and not red paint.

The second shot stung no less than the first, and Caleb rubbed it, wincing. He held up a hand towards the water tower, signaling defeat.

And then the faint sound of someone laughing. It was not coming from the water tower, and it was not Jackson, but it was *coming* from Jackson. And as Jackson approached, the laughing grew, and Caleb knew the laugh instantly.

Jackson produced the handheld radio with Parsons's laughter booming on the other end.

"You get all that?" Jackson said into the radio.

Parsons could only continue laughing.

Caleb did not smile inside this time. This time, his smile was on the outside and then some.

38

Harper was the sniper's name. When the man told Caleb this after his descent from the water tower, Caleb could not help but blurt: *"No shit?"* Though he primarily thought otherwise, tonight had Caleb thinking that there were no coincidences in the universe.

Harper, tall and thin, nearly gaunt, removed the baseball cap he was wearing, scratched his bald head, and frowned. "Something wrong?" he said.

Caleb held up a hand. "No, no, just"—he thought about explaining Harper the cat at Dylan's, but thought better of it—"never mind. You like Jackson here? *Just* Harper?"

"Craig," Harper said. "Jackson's first name is Sheldon. He hates it and insists on just Jackson."

"Asshole," Jackson said to Harper.

Caleb liked them already.

Parsons was still "in attendance," but now via FaceTime on Jackson's phone instead of the radio. It had taken Parsons nearly a minute to stop laughing, and then another two to bust Caleb's chops about his boys getting the best of him. Caleb had told Parsons what he'd told Jackson—that the smoke bomb could have been a real bomb, and that he could have shot Jackson—but Parsons was having none of it. Caleb let his friend have the moment.

Caleb eventually took Jackson's phone. "You told them everything?" he asked Parsons.

Parsons nodded. "Not a detail left out."

Caleb nodded back and then turned his attention towards Harper and Jackson, Harper's rifle back in its case and against the length of his leg, Jackson's Colt Python holstered.

"To say we don't have much time is an understatement," Caleb told them. "We've got three addresses we need to check. Fortunately, there are three of us. We can each stake out an address and then call the other two if we spot anything. This is a hit job, pure and simple. Any issues with morality I need to know about?"

"Nope," Jackson said.

Harper shook his head.

"Good. Can I assume your vehicles are holding more than you currently are?"

Both Jackson and Harper made faces as though insulted.

"Just saying it'll probably take more than paint," Caleb said.

"Just be happy it *was* paint," Harper said.

"And you be happy it was just smoke and not a—"

"*Shut up*," Parsons yelled from the phone.

Caleb and Harper shared a smile without smiling.

"Still, I've got gear in my car that we'll definitely need," Caleb said. "Top shelf, all of it."

Jackson lit a cigarette, exhaled, and said: "La-di-da."

"And just what is it that we'll definitely need?" Harper asked.

"Well, communication for one," Caleb said. "That radio you've got is fine"—he gestured towards the device now hooked to

Jackson's belt—"but if you guys plan on using both your hands tonight, I'd suggest headsets."

"What else?" Harper said.

"You'll see."

"We'll see? What is it, some kind of fucking surprise?"

"It's just shit that may come in handy, but won't weigh us down. We need to go in lean, not clunky. I recommend one sidearm and one long arm, but ultimately it's up to you, whatever you're most comfortable with. Hell, if I had my druthers, I'd let Harper find an ideal spot and pick them off one by one. Be home in time for breakfast."

"I can do that," Harper said.

"Assuming you find that ideal spot," Caleb countered.

"I always find at least one, champ."

"Well, let's just hope it's not as predictable as a fucking water tower."

"Jesus, you fucking guys," Parsons said. "I feel like I need to shout 'I'll turn this car around.'"

Three alphas in a room, Caleb thought. *The dick-measuring will never stop.* And part of Caleb didn't want it to. Much as a loner as Caleb typically was, he was enjoying this camaraderie that was under the guise of rivalry.

Caleb looked at the phone, at Parsons. "You send them the photos I gave you of Ogilvy?"

"I did."

Caleb looked at the two men. "Come through all right?"

Jackson said: "Crystal."

Harper nodded.

"He's the primary target," Caleb said, "but apparently he's protected with some decent muscle. Unfortunately, no photos of them, or anyone else who might be in attendance. So, basically kill anyone who looks like they need killing in one of those addresses."

Jackson took a final drag of his cigarette and flicked it into the night. "So, let's have the addresses," he said.

Caleb started to do just that, but got no further. Alexander's phone was vibrating in his back pocket.

39

In a lavish master bedroom with more square footage than a pricey one-bedroom apartment, Sam Ogilvy took the opportunity to call Alexander as Tatiana primped in the bathroom, it too none too shabby in size and extravagance.

Decker and Price sat at a nearby coffee table, playing cards. Two additional men stood outside the double doors of the bedroom, keeping guard. Four more downstairs, making considerable rounds throughout the vast palace of a home, and two standing guard outside by the front gate.

"Where the fuck are you?" Ogilvy said into the phone. "Call me back."

Decker and Price looked up from their card game.

"He's not answering," Ogilvy said.

Decker and Price rose from the table, started for the double doors.

Ogilvy held up a hand. "Wait, wait—hang on a second. He's sending a text."

Decker and Price looked on. Price popped the magazine on his pistol, a SIG Sauer P226, checked it, then slammed it back home.

"What's it say?" Decker asked.

Ogilvy relayed the exchange:

> Alexander: Tried answering but got nothing. Must be in a dead spot. This coming through okay?
>
> Ogilvy: I got it. How'd it go tonight?
>
> Alexander: Went well. Better than expected in fact.
>
> Ogilvy: How so?
>
> Alexander: Job's done and they had a little something extra on them as well.
>
> Ogilvy: Meaning what?
>
> Alexander: FAR more product than we'd anticipated.

Tatiana emerged from the bathroom wearing a negligee and a naughty smile. She could have walked any runway in New York City.

"*Not now*," Ogilvy said to her. "I'll call you when I'm ready."

Tatiana's naughty smile dropped. She turned and went back into the bathroom.

"And don't you dare fucking smoke while you're in there," he called to her. "I don't want to smell that shit on you when you come out."

"*More* product?" Decker said.

"That's what he wrote."

"What about Caleb?" Price asked.

> Ogilvy: Caleb gone?

Alexander: Gone.

"History," Ogilvy said to Price with a smile.

Price put his SIG Sauer away. He and Decker took their seats at the coffee table and resumed cards.

> Ogilvy: Give me a couple of hours. Meet us at the bar around twoish.

Alexander: Think I should come to you now. I made some calls after learning about the extra product. Got three prospective buyers willing to negotiate. Figured it best to give them an answer sooner than later.

> Ogilvy: They can wait. Meet at the bar. Twoish.

Alexander: You sure? One seemed keen to do it ASAP. Seemed willing to pay more than the norm.

> Ogilvy: Who is it?

"So, who is it?" Decker asked.

"Still waiting," Ogilvy said. "Taking his fucking time answering."

Alexander: Sorry. Some fucker nearly sideswiped us. Buyer is a new player. Name's Jackson.

> Ogilvy: Never heard of him. Forget it.

Alexander: Like I said, he's new. Can't hurt to look into it. He knows who we are. He'd be crazy to fuck with us. This could be big. I can be there ASAP. Who you with tonight?

> Ogilvy: Tatiana. Tell him if he's really interested then he'll just have to fucking wait. Bar at twoish.

40

Caleb looked at Jackson and Harper. "He wants to know who the buyer is. What do I say?"

"Tell him it's some new player in town," Jackson said. Caleb typed it. Even called the new player Jackson.

"Fuck," Caleb said. "Says he never heard of him and to forget it."

Parsons, who was still on Jackson's phone via FaceTime, said: "Tell him again that they're new players. Tell him they'd be crazy to fuck with us because of who we are and all that. Tell him it could be big and that you can be there ASAP. Ask what mistress he's with."

Caleb did.

"*Fuck!*" Caleb said again. "Said he's with some girl named Tatiana, but that the 'buyers' will just have to wait, the horny fucker."

"Okay, we've got a name," Harper said. "So where does Tatiana live?"

"How the hell should I know?" Caleb said. Then: "Wait. Wait, wait, wait . . ." Caleb scrolled through the list of contacts on

Alexander's phone, hoping beyond hope that when he got to the *T*'s…

"*Booyah!*" Caleb said. "Fucking Tatiana's number right here."

"So what?" Jackson said. "You planning on calling her and asking for directions?"

Don't do it, man.

"No, *Sheldon*," Caleb began, "but if I've got her number, I can all but guarantee you I've got her address."

"How's that?"

You swore you wouldn't.

Feeling a shame he had promised himself he wouldn't have to feel, Caleb pulled his own cell, sighed, and muttered: "*Shit.*"

41

Netflix night. A horror series they'd been hooked on about a vacationing family being stalked by psychos in the Florida Everglades.

Thomas Rose had already taken his spot on the couch—with a flop and a delighted sigh—and Faye was, to her insistence, preparing the popcorn in the kitchen.

After one bite, Thomas knew why.

"What is this?" he said. He hadn't even swallowed it all yet, looked in fact, like a kid ready to spit it back out with great disdain for the parent who had just fed him such ghastliness.

"Healthy Pop," Faye said. "Low calorie, low sodium, low fat."

"Low taste," Thomas said. He grimaced, swallowing down his recent mouthful. "It's like those packing-peanut things."

"Thomas…" she said, looking at him. Her Haitian accent, making *Thomas* sound like *Dhomas*, never failing to melt him, was enough. But the blue eyes (that Thomas would swear his wife had the supernatural ability to make bluer at will) she batted his way (and make no mistake; that batting was a mystical skill as well) was the coup de grâce. Thomas sat and ate Styrofoam peanuts during the show without further complaint.

Only he was saved when his cell phone rang, its ringtone—set to the theme of the original *Battlestar Galactica*—never failing to roll Faye's eyes.

"It's Caleb," he said before answering.

"Answer it then," Faye said quickly.

"Hello?" Close as they were, there was still a distance between Caleb and his staff, as though Caleb refused to get *too* close. It was for this reason that Thomas never answered with a "hey, man," or a "what's up, dude?" or any other such fraternal pleasantry.

"Thomas," Caleb said. "I lied; I need your help. I'm sorry, I really am, but—"

Apologizing? Caleb? Thomas thought. He must be desperate. And then: *Desperate? Caleb? Something must be very wrong.*

"It's fine, it's fine," Thomas said, cutting him off. "What is it?"

"The clock is ticking on this, so I need you to work fast," Caleb said. "Your gear powered up?"

"Always."

"I'm gonna read off two cell numbers. I need you to find me any interaction between the two tonight, and then the precise locations they originated from. Can you—I don't know what the hell you and Faye call it—*triangulate* the signals for me?"

"Actually, you'd call it—"

"*Thomas!*"

"On it." Thomas hurried up the stairs towards Faye's and his home office and took a seat in front of his main PC. "Okay, go."

Caleb gave him both Tatiana's and Ogilvy's cell numbers.

Thomas went to work, fingers clacking away, monitor flashing all sorts of code assuredly Greek to ninety percent of the population.

"Okay, I've only got one interaction from tonight. Checking locations on both cells…okay, one was from, wait…okay, one must have been from a car, because there are multiple locations within very short distances from one another."

"That's gotta be Ogilvy," Caleb said.

"Huh?"

"Forget it. The other location?"

"House in the Philly 'burbs. The Main Line to be exact. Affluent town called Berwyn. Waiting on a satellite map to confirm. Yup, big house in Berwyn. *Big* house. On the outskirts of town. Almost rural, but not, you know?"

"Don't care. Just give me the address."

"Texting it to you now."

Caleb felt his phone vibrate against his ear, looked at it, and saw the incoming text.

"Okay, got it," he said.

"Everything okay?" Thomas asked.

"Good job," was all Caleb said before he hung up.

Thomas needn't come downstairs to tell Faye what had transpired; she was watching and listening by the office door.

"What's going on?" she asked Thomas.

Thomas swiveled in his chair to face her. "I honestly have no idea. But he sounded a little desperate."

"Desperate? *Caleb?*" Faye said.

Déjà vu, Thomas thought.

42

"Who was that?" Jackson asked Caleb.

Caleb began fiddling with his phone. "Forget it. Give me your cell numbers, I'm texting you the address."

"So you got it?" Jackson said.

"I got it. Phone numbers."

Jackson and Harper gave them to Caleb. He sent them the address.

"Berwyn?" Harper said, looking at his phone.

"It's in the suburbs. Wealthy area called the Main Line. We're in luck, though—apparently it's a big house on the outskirts of town. No townhouse or cul-de-sac shit with prying eyes. Houses spaced far apart. We gotta hurry, though. He's expecting to meet us at the bar at twoish, but for all we know, he's a two-pump chump and might finish with Tatiana early, then make his way to the bar beforehand and see the mess I left."

"Why don't we just skip the house and go to the bar?" Jackson said. "Ambush him there?"

"I just said, I left one hell of a mess there."

"So? We can get them before they spot the mess."

Caleb thought about this for a moment. Then: "No—house gives us a better element of surprise. Plus we'll be able to spread out more efficiently. The bar is too close of quarters for my liking. We don't know their exact numbers. If it turns into a shootout, it could get messy."

Now Harper and Tucker thought for a moment.

"Plus, it's like I said earlier," Caleb began, "if Harper can pick them off from a distance, so much the better."

"Good as I am," Harper said, "I won't be able to get them all if they have greater numbers like you said."

"Just get as many as you can," Caleb said. "Jackson and I will play cleanup." He looked at Jackson. Jackson's face was ice. No confirmation needed.

"So, how exactly do you want to play it?" Harper asked.

Caleb told them. Both men approved.

"Follow me to my car," Caleb said. "I'll get us what we need."

43

Ogilvy rolled off of Tatiana. If he noticed, he did not seem to care about her dissatisfied expression. Ogilvy was as selfish a lover as he was a businessman.

Naked, Ogilvy stood and made his way towards his suit jacket draped over the chair Price had been using at the coffee table, Price and Decker no longer in the room as they had since joined the men downstairs in running surveillance of the house.

Ogilvy removed a pack of cigarettes from his jacket pocket and lit one.

"Why can you smoke, but I can't?" Tatiana asked.

"Why do you assume you can ask me something like that?" Ogilvy replied.

"Well, can I at least have one now?"

Ogilvy got back on the bed, sitting upright against the headboard. He took a deep drag to underline: "No. Fix me a drink first."

Tatiana huffed and got out of bed. Headed towards the small bar in the far corner of the bedroom, Ogilvy studying her naked body as she did so.

"You look like you've put on weight," he said to her.

Tatiana stopped cold and faced him.

"Just because I keep you in luxury doesn't give you an excuse to be lazy," Ogilvy said. "You have certain obligations to me. One of them—the primary one—is to keep yourself tight."

Tatiana went to reply, but appeared to think better of it.

"You're expendable," Ogilvy said. "Never forget that."

Tatiana finally spoke. "I've been working out every day."

"Work harder, or else someone else will be sleeping in this bed before long."

Tatiana dropped her head, nodded, then turned back towards the bar and started fixing Ogilvy his drink.

She returned to the bed with a Glenfiddich 30 Year Old neat and handed it to him.

"Can I have a cigarette now?" she asked.

"Will it blunt your appetite?"

"I—yes."

"Then take the whole pack."

44

The two men stood guard outside the iron gates. Behind them, *far* behind them, down the cobblestone driveway, was a home fit for a king. Or, in this instance, a queen.

If one were to happen upon the two men standing before those iron gates on foot, they might think the home was the only one for miles. This was where Thomas's earlier statement to Caleb about the area being more rural than suburban became fitting—each home was countless yards apart; each home, nestled deep within its wooded environs.

But that was where Thomas's analogy ended. There were no stereotypical country homes here. Nothing dating back centuries, built with strong backs and pride. No, these homes were built with pens, unashamed in their ostentatiously modern design amongst the bucolic surroundings.

But of course there would be no one happening by on foot, especially at this time of night. But a car? A car was not out of the realm of possibility. Certainly not a car that had lost its way throughout the poorly lit back roads and endless miles of forested panorama on either side.

CALEB: ATONEMENT

And so as the two men standing guard before the iron gates argued over which the better mob film was—*The Godfather* or *Goodfellas*—their alarm bells did not sound too loudly when headlights slowly approached.

When the headlights rolled to a stop before them? The alarm bells grew louder, though nothing deafening. After all, only a fool looking to cause trouble would be so blatant in his approach.

———

CALEB "THE FOOL" Lambert, rolled down his driver's side window, smiled at the two men, and said: "Tatiana live here?"

Clearly not the brightest of bulbs—the alarm bells should have been screaming now—the two men exchanged a curious look before one said: "What business you got with her?"

"None." Caleb shot them both in the head, the muffled *pop! pop!* of the Glock's suppressor echoing throughout the wooded night around them.

Caleb killed the engine and got out of his vehicle.

"The guy she's fucking…?" he said to the two dead men as he began dragging them away from the iron gates and towards some nearby foliage. "*That's* the fella I've got some business with. Don't suppose you've got a key to the house, do you?"

Caleb patted down both men. One had a ring of keys. Caleb groaned. "I suppose it would have been too easy if you had just *one* key, wouldn't it? Oh well, I guess I should just be grateful you two guys are—sorry—*were* as stupid as you were."

Caleb hopped back into his car. Drove a hundred yards down the road and killed his engine again. He put his headset on.

"You guys with me?" he said.

"Here," Jackson said.

"Yep," Harper said.

"The two guys at the gate are down. I got their keys, but who knows which is for where; there's a lot. Jackson, I'm a hundred yards east of the gate. Meet me there now. Harper, impress me and tell me you found that ideal spot."

"I did. Fifty yards west as the crow flies. Woods. Good cover."

"You in position?"

"Not yet. Give me ten before you and Jackson make a move. I'll get as many as I can. Like I said before, though; chances are I won't be able to get them all if they've got decent numbers. If that happens, you'll need to move fast playing cleanup."

"Just get as many as you can," Caleb said for the second time tonight. "However, Jackson and I are gonna have to move now to check viable entrances with the keys. If we get lucky, we won't head inside until you're ready, though."

"What about alarm systems?" Harper asked.

"I'm hoping there isn't one."

"No way a house like this doesn't have an alarm."

"Then I'm hoping it isn't armed. They're inside. I've known countless people who never arm their systems when they're home and awake. Only before going to bed, or leaving the house. They're doing neither."

"And if it *is* armed?" Jackson asked.

"Got that covered," Caleb said.

"How's that?"

"Portable EMP."

"*Portable* EMP?"

"Yep. Saved Chip's ass in Noodle. Delivers a strong spike of multispectrum interference. Should disable all tech systems. Alarms, cameras, lights…"

"I know what an EMP does," Jackson said.

"So then you wanna take back your 'la-di-da' comment about the top-shelf gear in my car?"

"No."

Caleb smiled. "Like I said, it'll disable the lights too. You got night vision on your scope, Harper?"

"I do."

"Baller. If the alarm *is* armed, and we're forced to use the EMP, killing the lights will give us another distinct advantage. What's the clarity on your night vision? You won't be shooting us by mistake, will you?"

"Not a chance. It's not thermal. You'll be black and white, that's all."

"Love it. Jackson, any chance your long arm is cozying up to a tactical light?"

"Of course."

"La-di-da."

"Won't the EMP zap neighboring homes?" Harper asked.

"It shouldn't," Caleb replied. "It's a portable EMP, the size of a remote control, nothing crazy. Range isn't that far."

"What about our headsets?" Jackson asked.

"Battery operated," Caleb said. "EMP won't touch them."

Jackson mumbled something under his breath. The final la-di-da, if Caleb had to bet, and he smiled again.

"Getting into position," Harper said.

"Copy that," Caleb said. "Jackson, see you in a few. Listen, if we all die tonight, I want you guys to know that it was nice meeting you."

"The hell kind of talk is that?" Harper said.

"You guys don't know me that well yet," Caleb replied. "I'm kinda fucked up."

45

Caleb's car was parked on the side of the road, one hundred yards east of the house. He stood by the trunk, waiting.

Jackson pulled up behind him moments later. Exited his vehicle and approached.

"You feel that?" Caleb asked.

"Feel what?" Jackson said, voice gravelly as ever.

"That tingle."

"Tingle?"

Caleb knew Jackson would never feel *his* particular tingle, but guessed there might be something close. He likened Jackson and Harper to soldiers who feared domestic life more than war. It was why they were here with him now, embracing their born purpose, their own tingle, long after retirement.

"Down to your plums," Caleb said. "Like someone's dragging a feather over them."

Caleb could see that Jackson got it, but still he said: "You really *are* fucked up, aren't you?"

"I am, yes," Caleb said. "But I'm reliable."

Caleb popped his trunk.

"More la-di-da?" Jackson said.

"Flash, smoke, and frag grenades, yes. Vests, no." Caleb pulled a vest from the trunk and handed it to Jackson.

Jackson handed it back.

"What's wrong?" Caleb asked.

"No vests," Jackson said.

"Why not?"

"Don't like 'em."

"What?"

"You worry about getting shot, you *get* shot," Jackson said. "Never wore a vest in all my years on duty."

"You ever been shot?"

"Yeah."

"Well, then what the hell?"

"Not wearing a vest," Jackson said again.

"Dude, this is foreshadowing 101, for fuck's sake. Please take the vest so I don't get to have the pleasure of telling your corpse I told you so."

"No."

Caleb shook his head. "Fine. What about the grenades? Got some kind of superstitious BS with them too?"

"No—I'll take those."

Caleb handed Jackson one of each. Jackson tucked the flashbang and the smoke grenade into his pack bag, but handed back the frag.

"So, you *do* have some superstitious BS," Caleb said.

"I got no problems with frags, except when it comes to close quarters."

Touché, Caleb thought, though he'd never concede the point. Still, he said: "Harper took one."

"And Craig is outside, fifty yards away, according to him."

Touché, touché. Yet he still refused to concede. "Suit yourself."

"I will. And I'll thank you to follow my lead. Be a damn shame if you blew up the house with us in it."

Caleb smiled, then gestured towards Jackson's pack bag, where he'd just stuffed the smoke and flashbang. "Know how to use them?" he asked.

"You know how to use your pecker?"

"Depends on who you ask, I guess."

Jackson snorted, either amused by Caleb's quip, or lacking respect for it; Caleb couldn't tell—Jackson's bearded, stony face was not an easy read, even for Caleb.

Caleb started to put on the vest Jackson had refused. "Well, I for one do not like the sensation of bullets piercing my flesh. And I hope this too is foreshadowing."

"*Pussy,*" Jackson said behind a cough.

"Was that *levity* from Sheldon Jackson? Shame it's dark; I'd look up to see the pigs flying."

"You're a weird dude, man. And call me Sheldon again and that vest won't help you."

"Stop—you're scaring me." Caleb shut the trunk. "Weapons check."

Both men checked their side- and long arm. Jackson's sidearm was his familiar Colt Python .357.

"You really going in with a six-shooter?" Caleb asked.

"Yup," Jackson said, checking the open barrel of his Python before palming it back in with a definitive click.

"You at least got a speed loader for it?" Caleb asked.

Jackson patted the pack bag at his side. "I do."

"Well, that's something, I guess." Caleb checked the magazine in his Glock before palming it back in himself. He then checked the magazines fixed to one side of his belt.

Jackson went into his pack bag and checked said speed loaders.

Caleb holstered his Glock and checked his long arm, a carbine version of the SIG SG 550 with a suppressor, designed for close-quarter combat. Checked its current ammo and the additional magazines fixed on the opposite side of his belt. He then clicked the tactical light fixed to the rifle on and off three times. Repeated the same ritual with a small but powerful flashlight, no bigger than a Magic Marker, before fixing it back to his belt alongside the additional magazines.

Jackson did the same, his long arm the traditional—of course—AK-47, it too equipped with a suppressor and tactical light, it too excelling in close-quarter combat due to its penetration and stopping power over its lifelong rival, the M-16.

Finished, Caleb asked again: "Feeling the tingle yet?"

Jackson finally caved. "Maybe a little."

"Wish I felt okay saying the N-word," Caleb said. "I'd say, 'my… you know.'"

"Huh?"

"You ever see *Training Day*? Denzel Washington? He kept saying, 'my…you know.'"

"I saw *Training Day*. Why can't you say it?"

"A—because I don't like the word. And B—it always sounds incredibly lame coming from a white boy."

Jackson stuck out his lower lip and nodded. "True."

"Shall we go and get our tingle on then?" Caleb said.

"What about those keys?" Jackson asked.

"It's like I said earlier; there's like ten of them on the ring. When we find a decent entry point, we'll have to hope our first pick of keys is gold before we're spotted."

"Why not just forget the keys and use the portable EMP? Fry everything, then kick the fucking door down."

"Ever see *Colors*?" Caleb asked. "Late '80s movie with Sean Penn and Robert Duvall? They're cops in gangland areas of Los Angeles that—"

"I saw *Colors*. You watch a lot of movies."

"Says the guy who's seen both films I mentioned."

"I've got about forty years on you. Plus I was retired for a spell. What's your excuse?"

Caleb frowned and shook away Jackson's point. "Whatever. Anyway, there's a scene where Sean Penn, the rookie cop, is getting overzealous, wants to rush in and all that. Robert Duvall, the senior, experienced cop, tells Penn a story about two bulls on a hill looking down on a bunch of cows. The younger bull suggests running down and fucking one of the cows. But the wiser, older bull suggests it's better to *walk* down and fuck them all."

"I said I saw the film."

"Then would you agree that hitting the portable EMP and kicking the door down would be akin to running down the hill to fuck just one cow, as opposed to using the keys, walking on in, and then fucking them all?"

Jackson hesitated, Caleb's logic putting him on the ropes. His ego, however, would not allow him to fully yield without a desperation haymaker. "Assuming the alarm isn't armed. If it is, we'll have no *choice* but to use the EMP."

"You made an effort with levity. How about a little optimism?"

"How about we fucking move before Harper starts to think we bailed on him."

"Fair enough."

"Fun time's over," Jackson said, gripping his AK-47 tight in both hands.

Caleb gripped his SIG SG 550 tight in both hands as well. "Optimism, Sheldon. Fun's just about to start."

46

Harper was in place, fifty yards west as the crow flies, just as he'd said. And again, as he said, his cover was solid. Woods with good underbrush for camouflage.

Peering through the custom scope of his M24 SWS, Harper zeroed in on the house, in particular its many windows, looking for signs of movement. The exceptional make of the custom scope was such that one might feel they could reach out and touch whatever it happened upon.

Harper hoped he would be able to reach out and touch many.

So far, however, he had yet to do so, but patience for the sniper was a learned attribute as vital as proficiency in operating the weapon itself.

"You guys with me?" Harper spoke into his headset.

"We're with you," Caleb whispered. "You in position?"

"Yup. House is crystal. No signs of movement inside yet. What's your position?"

"Jackson and I hopped the wall on the east side of the house. Well, I hopped; Jackson not so much."

"Fuck you," Jackson whispered back.

"We're going to try entry by the patio overlooking the pool first," Caleb said. "Sliding glass doors. No signs of movement here either, but it's dark inside. What's your light situation?"

"Downstairs is primarily dark. Upstairs is decently lit."

"That means he's still up there with his queen," Caleb said. "Probably has his men close by."

"He'd be foolish not to have someone patrolling the downstairs," Harper replied. "He had the two guys at the gate."

"True," Caleb said. "But I'd wager he's not on any considerable alert. Far as he knows, the job went well, and I'm dead."

"Check the key on the sliding glass doors and get back to—*wait*, I've got movement."

"Upstairs or downstairs? Upstairs or downstairs?"

"Upstairs. Someone just passed one of the windows."

"Was it Ogilvy?"

"Couldn't tell; he didn't loiter."

"Don't suppose you've got a view of the master bedroom?" Caleb asked.

"Can't tell that either. Blinds are drawn on some of the windows."

"Fuck," Caleb said.

"Blinds drawn would indicate a need for privacy," Jackson said.

"Well aware," Harper said. "But unless they feel like stargazing, I imagine they're staying closed for the night. Get to work on the keys. Switching to night vision to cover your movement."

"Stand by," Caleb said.

47

A knock on the double doors of the master bedroom.
"Come in."
Decker and Price entered. Ogilvy was still on the bed, sipping the scotch Tatiana had poured him. He had yet to get dressed, unashamed of his nakedness in front of his men.

Tatiana stood by the bar, smoking a cigarette and sipping a Ketel One on the rocks she'd poured for herself. She'd since put on a red silk robe, more so to hide her figure from Ogilvy's critical eye as opposed to any one of Ogilvy's men who might enter.

"What time do you want to get moving?" Decker asked.

Ogilvy drained the last of his scotch, then held up the empty glass and wiggled it in Tatiana's direction without looking at her.

"I told Alexander we'd meet him at the bar around two," Ogilvy said.

Tatiana took his glass, went back to the bar, refilled it, and then brought it back. Again, Ogilvy did not look at her as he took his drink. Did not thank her.

"It's a little after one," Decker said. "Might want to get moving soon."

"He can fucking wait," Ogilvy said.

"You think it was strange he never called?" Decker asked.

"Said his signal was shit," Ogilvy said. "He texted all we needed to know."

Now Price chimed in. "He seemed eager about this potential new buyer. You'd think he'd call once he got a better signal."

Ogilvy sipped his scotch. "So, what are you guys saying?"

Price shrugged. "Just doesn't feel right to me."

"Me neither," Decker added.

"Alexander wouldn't dare fuck me."

"No," Price said, shaking his head, "not that. Just..."

"Just *what?*"

"Just something doesn't feel right," Price said again.

Ogilvy sighed and grabbed his phone from the nightstand. Called Alexander. Waited.

"No answer?" Decker asked.

Ogilvy frowned and hung up. "Voicemail," he said.

Decker and Price exchanged a look.

"Just what the fuck is he up to?" Ogilvy said to himself. Then to his men: "You think he'd be stupid enough to try and make a deal with this new buyer without me?"

"I think you're barking up the wrong tree here, boss," Decker said.

"Meaning what exactly?"

"Meaning I wonder if it was actually Alexander who was texting you tonight."

Ogilvy frowned again. Went to say something but stopped, mouth open—the phone in his hand had just vibrated.

"He sent another text."

Price started to speak, but Ogilvy held up a hand, silencing him. Ogilvy immediately began to text Alexander back. Finished, he looked up at Decker and Price.

"What'd it say?" Price asked.

"Said something was up with his phone. Said he answered but couldn't get anything. Said text was the only thing working."

"And you said?"

"I told him it all sounded like a crock of shit. I told him if he was up to something I'd mail his balls to his wife."

"Ask him—"

The phone vibrated again. And Ogilvy raised a hand, silencing Price again.

"Says: 'Not up to anything at all. Swear on my life. My phone truly is fucked up for some reason. Let's just meet at the bar and I'll explain everything there.'"

Ogilvy hopped out of bed and started to get dressed.

"Wait," Price said.

Ogilvy had just—mercifully for Decker and Price—put on his underwear, then started on his pants when he said: "What?"

"Text him back and ask him something," Price said. "Something only Alexander would know."

48

"F*uck*," Caleb whispered. "Alexander's phone is ringing again."

Caleb and Jackson were on the blind side of the sliding glass door that sported the lock, tight to the adjacent wall. They had tried two keys thus far to no avail when Alexander's phone had started buzzing.

"Don't answer," Jackson said.

"Really? Because I was just about to so I could say hi."

Jackson gave him a look.

When the phone stopped ringing, Caleb started to send a text.

"What are you doing?" Jackson whispered.

"Texting him. Telling him the phone is screwed up for some reason. That text is all that's working."

"He's not gonna buy it this time," Jackson said. "Just leave it and let's try the other keys."

"Too late," Caleb said. "Just sent the text."

The phone vibrated a minute later.

"Okay," Caleb said, reading the text. "Okay."

"Okay, what?"

"Well, he's not buying the broken phone thing, but—"

"Told you—"

"*But* he still thinks it's Alexander. Thinks he's up to something shady." Caleb started texting a reply.

"Now what are you writing?" Jackson asked.

"I'm telling him nothing fishy is up and that the phone really is being weird. Telling him we'll meet him at the bar to explain."

"This is flat-out dumb," Jackson said. "Forget the fucking phone and let's just get inside."

"What's going on?" Harper said into their headsets.

"Hang on a sec," Caleb said to Harper.

The phone vibrated again. "*Fuuuck*," Caleb said.

"What?" Jackson said.

Caleb looked at Jackson. "He just sent a text asking me what his wife's name was."

"*Told* you," Jackson said. "The guy is on to us."

Caleb stared at the text without seeing it, his mind racing, calculating.

"*Just keep trying the keys!*" Jackson said in a loud whisper.

Caleb pocketed the phone and did as Jackson suggested.

Third key. Nope.

Fourth key. Nope.

The phone vibrated again. Caleb pulled it from his pocket.

"*Fucking leave it!*" Jackson whispered loudly again.

"Says: 'Wife's name. NOW.'"

"Give me the goddamn keys," Jackson said.

Caleb handed them over. Jackson let his AK-47 hang by its shoulder strap as he took the keys and went to work.

Fifth key. Nope.

Sixth key. Nope.

Seventh and final key.

"*Fuck!*" Jackson said. "None of them work."

"Gotta be for another door then."

"If for any door here at all," Jackson said. "They could be the dude's own personal keys, for all we know."

Caleb looked at the text again. "Wife's name. NOW."

Something delicious threatened Caleb's better judgment.

Don't do it.

Caleb's thumbs hovered over the phone's keyboard, twitching.

Don't do it.

He glanced up at Jackson. "Looks like we might have to run down that hill after all."

"Fine with me."

"Can't let any of the cows get away, though."

"Then we better fuck 'em fast."

"Oh, I do like you, Sheldon."

"We survive this, and I'm kicking the shit out of you."

"*Optimism*, Sheldon—you'll be kicking the shit out of me in no time. Harper, you getting all this?"

"I am," Harper replied. "What do you have in mind?"

"We're going with the EMP," Caleb said. "Gonna zap everything, shoot out the glass, and then it's on. You hit anything moving that isn't us."

"Roger that."

"Just keep in mind that it's a *portable* EMP," Caleb said. "Powerful but not *that* powerful. The effect will be temporary; it doesn't truly fry everything. Power will eventually come back on."

"*How* temporary?" Jackson said.

"It varies, depending on the target. Let's hope longer than shorter."

Caleb pulled the portable EMP from his own pack bag at his side, and then handed it to Jackson. Jackson made a curious face that was an easy read: *Why you giving the EMP to* me?

"Give me one sec," Caleb said to Jackson as he started to text, giving Ogilvy an answer in regard to his wife's name.

What the hell is the point? Don't do it.

But much like Caleb had changed Nick's caller ID from "Nick" to "Secretary" in order to appreciate the little things in life, so too was his eternally warped sense of humor adamant in enjoying the little things here and now. After all, for someone as colossally damaged as he would always be, for Caleb, the little things were all he had.

His text reply to Ogilvy was "Widow."

Caleb then pocketed the phone, clicked on the tactical light fixed to his SIG SG 550, looked at Jackson, and said: "Zap 'em."

49

Barefoot and shirtless, Ogilvy made fists with his impatient toes in the carpet as he stared at his phone, waiting for a reply from someone who may or may not have been Alexander.

Price had once again pulled his SIG Sauer P226 and instinctively checked its magazine again. Decker did the same with his Beretta 92FS.

Satisfied, both men holstered their guns and then pulled their beloved knives. No ammo to check on those, but as instinctive as it was for them to check the ammo on their pistols, despite previous checks, so too was it instinctive, if not comforting, to finger the blades to ensure they were as razor sharp as ever. When both men drew blood on their index fingers, they were once again satisfied.

"Put those away," Ogilvy said, gesturing towards the knives. "If this isn't Alexander, then I think it's safe to assume it's Caleb. And if it is, I don't want you guys having any 'fun.' He's not the type you play with."

Both men slid their knives back into the leather sheaths hanging from their belts.

Decker rubbed his hand vigorously over his shaved head. One might think it was a pacifying gesture he used when anxious. Truth was, he did it when he was excited, the way Price tugged at his earlobe when he too was excited. Only now, Price's earlobe was safe—he sucked the blood from his index finger instead, almost sensually. Foreplay.

"Okay, here we go," Ogilvy said. "Three dots. He's typing something."

Decker and Price looked on like dogs hoping to be fed.

"*Motherfucker*," Ogilvy hissed.

"What? *What?*" Price said.

Ogilvy looked up. "He wrote 'widow.'"

Price and Decker glanced at one another, the subtlest of smiles on their faces. They were going to be fed.

"It's him, isn't it?" Ogilvy said. "It's Caleb."

Both Price and Decker went to reply in the affirmative, but never got that far.

Their world was suddenly black.

50

Both Caleb and Jackson shot through the sliding glass doors, surrounding glass spider-webbing out from the holes.

They did not leap through the splintered glass in a theatric dive and roll (nor did anyone with a brain), just kicked out enough to shoulder their way through.

Their rifles were high and steady, flashlights on the rifles piercing the darkness as they crept.

A shadow rounded the corner. Caleb aimed, flashlight momentarily blinding the shadow. A quick burst of shots—*pop! pop! pop! pop!* Three to the body, one to the head.

One down.

Moving faster now through what appeared to be the den. Sounds of commotion from above.

Another shadow rounded the corner, Jackson's tactical light on his rifle betraying his whereabouts, the shadow firing his weapon without a suppressor, the sound deafening, the shots missing Jackson, the two then clashing, engaged in an upright grapple, desperate to free their weapons as they fought.

Jackson headbutted the shadow, then brought his knee up into his groin, the shadow groaning, Jackson shoving him away, raising his rifle to shoot, ending up not having to as his flashlight illuminated the spectacle of the man's head exploding a split-second prior, blood and bits spraying Jackson's face.

"Thanks," Jackson whispered to Harper. He wiped away the blood and bits. "I think."

"Two coming down the staircase," Harper replied. "*These* two have lights. Advantage even now."

"Balls," Caleb said.

With no prior layout of the house's considerable interior, the staircase was not an immediate find.

"Keep heading south," Caleb told Jackson, "I've got east."

51

Jackson continued south, through the den.

Caleb went east, found the foyer and the staircase. He spotted the two men descending, lights bobbing, one of the men getting shots off before Caleb, two of the shots catching Caleb in the chest, his vest preventing injury, but slowing him a second, taking his wind. He backpedaled rapidly, finding cover behind the wall he'd just emerged from.

Sounds of broken glass, a *sha-thunk!*, and then the unmistakable sound of a body hitting the tiled floor. Caleb peeked from behind the wall. One of the men on the stairs was now facedown on the tiles, the top half of his head missing.

Two for Harper.

Three down in total. How many more?

The second man on the stairs opened fire on the wall Caleb was using for cover, getting off multiple rounds, his rifle too without a suppressor, the sound equally as deafening as before.

The drywall was weak cover, the bullets finding their way through. Caleb dropped low, considered a leopard crawl—belly to the ground, driving himself forward with his elbows and knees—

back into the foyer to minimize himself as a target and catch the man on the stairs, thought better of it, and then scuttled further away from the foyer and into the dining room. Let the fucker come to him.

Caleb took quick inventory of the dining room, found what he was after, and then flicked off his rifle's light.

Come into my parlor, said the spider to the fly.

52

Sounds of the suppressor on Jackson's AK-47 firing, the all-too-familiar sounds of a suppressor-free rifle firing back. Jackson was clearly in a firefight with someone.

The man on the stairs? Caleb thought.

No. After seeing what Harper did to the first one, the second would not be keen to loiter. Besides, the stairs would provide lousy cover; Jackson would take him easily.

So, that meant two downstairs now?

As though reading Caleb's mind, Jackson, forced to whisper yell over the gunfire: *"One appeared from the north end of the foyer! Could be multiple staircases! The one on the main staircase is gone!"*

And then, as if on cue, the second man from the stairs appeared in the dining room and started spraying it with gunfire, windows shattering, tall curtains adjacent to the windows billowing, dining room table coming apart in chunks, surrounding drywall filling with holes.

When the gunfire stopped, the man crept forward to inspect his work. Dropped low and shined his rifle's light under the dining room table. Rose but did not bother to check the curtains; if someone were hiding behind them, they would have tumbled out by now.

"*Psst!*"

The man spun.

Perched high atop the enormous armoire, to the immediate left of the dining room's entryway, sat Caleb, legs dangling over the armoire's ledge, not unlike a child's.

And the analogy was apt; Caleb felt the glee of a child when the man did not immediately open fire up at Caleb, but instead opened his mouth in disbelief, and Caleb, now wielding his Glock in one hand and his tactical flashlight in the other, actually managed his first shot into that open mouth.

He fired down three more into the man's torso for insurance, and was now shamefully hopeful that he, Jackson, and Harper would live through this for more than the obvious reason. The bragging rights on an open-mouth shot would be priceless.

53

Jackson and his assailant, roughly ten yards apart in the foyer, exchanged periodic bursts of fire from behind their respective walls.

When his rifle clicked empty, Jackson popped it, let it fall to the floor, slammed in another, and resumed firing.

It became a futile game of give and take. They were getting nowhere.

Fuck this, Jackson thought. He reached into his pack bag, pulled the flashbang, pulled the pin, waited for the assailant's gunfire to momentarily pause, and then rolled the stun grenade towards his foe.

The flashbang's impact was great enough to make even Jackson's vision swim for a moment after the thunderous sound and burst of light cleared, yet he wasted little time in rushing forward, appearing before his disoriented assailant like a phantom.

The shine of Jackson's light on his AK might have momentarily blinded the assailant...if he wasn't already blind from the flashbang. In the black of whatever the hell room they were in now, Jackson shined the light on the man's chest and ripped off at least ten rounds, the man's chest opening up like a party favor as he flew backwards, dead before he hit the floor.

54

"One more down," Jackson said into his headset.

"So I noticed," Caleb replied. The explosion of light from the flashbang all but lit the entire first floor of the house. No easy feat given its size.

One more for Jackson, and one more for Caleb. That made five down. How many freaking more were there? More importantly, were any of them Ogilvy? It was hard to tell in the gloom of the house.

"Got me another too," Caleb said. "Don't suppose yours was Ogilvy?"

"No," Jackson said. "Harper got one, though. Couldn't tell if it was Ogilvy. Part of his head was gone."

"Harper actually got *two*," Caleb said. "Guy I saw was missing a face as well. Harper, you there? You spot Ogilvy yet? Harper…?"

55

Harper, flat on his belly fifty yards west, peered through his scope. His surroundings did not exist—his whole world was inside that scope.

He'd gotten two thus far with little trouble. Had monitored a good deal of Jackson and Caleb's movement throughout the downstairs of the home with little trouble.

Upstairs was still a hurdle. The bulk of the windows still had the blinds drawn, and the windows that didn't had failed to show anything, particularly Ogilvy.

He'd heard Jackson's claim that there was likely a second staircase, but damned if he could spot it. Perhaps Ogilvy had used that second staircase to flee? No. Chances were solid he would have spotted him making an exit from downstairs, and chances were more than solid that he would have spotted headlights of a fleeing car from the driveway.

That meant Ogilvy was still upstairs somewhere, likely being protected by the highly trained men Caleb had alluded to earlier; the men he, Jackson, and Caleb had dispatched thus far were too overzealous in their attack, lacked proper awareness and precaution.

"Come on, come on..." Harper whispered to himself, willing someone else to appear.

Someone did, but it was the total antithesis of Harper's will.

A crack of a branch behind him, and Harper pulled his eye from the scope, went to roll onto his back, but never made it.

A firm hand slapped itself over his forehead and jerked his whole head back. Harper saw the brief flash of the blade a second before it slashed his throat.

56

"Bunch of sly foxes you guys are, aren't ya?" Decker said, sheathing his blade while he looked down on the dying sniper.

Decker then rolled the sniper's body away, got down onto his own belly, and pressed his eye into the scope of the rifle.

The sniper gargled blood beside him.

"Let's see what we can see, yeah?" Decker said. "Damn good scope, my man. Love me some night vision."

Decker spotted Caleb and another man with a beard in the foyer, regrouping.

"Too easy," Decker said, grinning. He rubbed his hand back and forth over his shaved head and started to sing "A-Hunting We Will Go."

57

Flat on his back, choking on his own blood, Harper felt himself fading. The night sky was narrowing in a circle like the end of an old "Looney Tunes" cartoon he'd loved so much as a kid. He was not naïve enough to think that the trademark *"That's all folks!"* at the end of those cartoons would also be applying to him soon as well.

In his headset, which he couldn't answer: "Harper, you there? You spot Ogilvy yet? Harper...?"

With as little movement as possible, Harper reached into his pack bag at his side.

Next to him, looking through the custom scope of *his* M24 SWS (Harper's first wife had had an affair; the man next to him, having an affair with his M24 SWS, hurt more), the man started to sing:

"A-hunting we will go,
A-hunting we will go
Heigh-ho, the derry-o,
A-hunting we will go.

A-hunting we will go,
A-hunting we will go
We'll catch a fox and put him in a box
And never let him go."

"Harper! Where the fuck are you?"

Harper pulled the frag grenade from his pack bag. Pulled the pin.

58

Decker stopped singing. Caleb's head was smack center in his crosshairs. Better to do him first.

He placed the pad of his index finger gently on the trigger. No stranger to sniping himself, Decker slowly breathed in, breathed out, and then held it, looking for his natural respiratory pause, the most stable moment of the breathing cycle.

The dying man next to him suddenly rolled his way. And again, being no stranger to sniping himself, knowing the benefits of keeping *both* eyes open while shooting, Decker picked up the dying man's movement in the peripheral vision of his eye unoccupied with the scope.

Decker turned his head towards the dying man. He was not overly alarmed. He had slashed the man deep; it was likely a desperate attempt at grabbing the rifle to disrupt his shot before he truly died.

When the dying man grinned a mouthful of blood and brandished the live frag, Decker was alarmed.

"Ahhh shit," he said.

59

Caleb and Jackson had momentarily regrouped in the foyer.

"Why the fuck isn't he answering?" Caleb said.

"No idea."

"*Harper!*" Caleb whisper yelled. "*Where the fuck are you?*"

"Fuck this," Jackson said. "I'm going upstairs." He started to move.

"*Wait!*" Caleb whisper yelled again. "*We need Harper's cover!*"

An explosion boomed in their headsets, causing both men to jerk, wince, and then rip their headsets off and toss them away.

Ears ringing, still wincing, Caleb and Jackson exchanged panicked looks, then bolted towards the west end of the downstairs. Found themselves in the living room. Looked out one of the many windows and, aided by the moonlight, could just make out the cloud of smoke in the wooded area beyond...roughly fifty yards away.

"Fuck!" No whisper yell for Jackson. His friend was gone. "Why would they blow him up?"

"They didn't," Caleb said, confident in his notion. "He blew himself up. Took someone with him too."

Jackson looked at Caleb.

"Ogilvy's men would never draw attention to themselves like that. Someone found Harper's spot, got the drop on him, and Harper managed to pull a Hail Mary with a frag." Saying it aloud, Caleb was now certain his notion was fact.

Jackson studied Caleb. Caleb could see the notion resonating as fact with Harper too. Perhaps more so than it had with Caleb. Jackson knew Harper inside and out. Knew his friend would sacrifice his own life to save them.

Jackson's stony face contorted into the rare spectacle of sorrow. It was short-lived, however; vengeance immediately replaced that sorrow, an expression Caleb knew all too well. He only hoped that vengeance wouldn't cause Jackson to become careless.

And then, as though heaven sent, there was movement behind them. A tactical light appeared, its neighboring rifle opening fire.

Both dove away from the window, the rifle obliterating the glass.

Jackson took cover behind a sofa, Caleb a second sofa.

Jackson pulled his smoke bomb and rolled it towards the shooter. The grenade popped and hissed, the room instantly full of thick smoke. Even the shooter's tactical light could not penetrate it.

Jackson pulled his Colt Python. Stood and walked—didn't run —towards where the shooter had been standing.

Caleb looked on through the now dissipating smoke, still aided by the moonlight behind him.

He found himself thinking for the second time tonight that there were no coincidences. Jackson's need for vengeance. An enemy appearing. Neither he nor Jackson taking a hit. Jackson throwing smoke, rising and *walking* through the cloak of the smoke, now finding his man with no trouble, latching onto the man's shoulder with one hand, jamming the barrel of his Colt into the man's throat with the other, pulling the trigger twice before the man could raise his rifle again, the man's legs buckling as he gurgled, but Jackson holding on to his shoulder, keeping his slumping body upright with the adrenalized strength rage gives us all, now ramming the barrel of his Colt into the man's gut, firing three more times, finally letting go, allowing the man to drop before bending over his dying body, spitting on him, and then using the final bullet in his Colt to blast the man between the eyes.

One more for Harper,

(rest in peace, brother)

and one more for Jackson, Caleb thought. *That's seven down now. Where the* hell *is Ogilvy?*

Jackson turned away from his man and approached Caleb, his face back to its stony self. If you asked Caleb, vengeance beat Prozac any fucking day of the week.

Still, Caleb asked: "You okay?"

"Don't wanna talk about it," Jackson replied.

"Fine. Don't have time anyway. That frag definitely woke up the neighborhood. We gotta do what we came to do and get the hell outta here before *real* police turn up."

"How do you want to play it?" Jackson asked, pulling a speed loader from his pack bag and reloading his Colt.

"Ogilvy's in here somewhere."

"Could have left."

Caleb shook his head. "Harper would have spotted him. Either picked him off himself or told us before he—" Caleb caught himself, broke eye contact with Jackson for a beat, cursed his shoddy filter, then resumed with: "He would have told us."

Jackson said nothing.

"Head outside," Caleb said. "Stake out the driveway. I don't think I need to tell you what to do if someone tries to leave."

"We should be equally worrying about arrivals," Jackson said. "I'm talking about the 'real' police you mentioned. The good guys."

"Headsets," Caleb said.

They went back into the foyer, picked up the headsets they'd torn off after Harper's frag had assaulted their ears, and put them back on.

"Got me?" Caleb said, testing the headset.

"Got you. You got me?"

Caleb nodded. "You see any flashing lights approaching, you let me know, then get the hell out of here."

"What about you? You'll get the hell out of here too, yeah?"

"Not until I find Ogilvy."

Jackson studied Caleb.

"Optimism, Jackson." No way was he going to call him Sheldon again. Not after what happened to Harper.

The electricity suddenly came back on. Appliances hummed; light on the second floor could be seen from the gloom of the foyer.

"So much for optimism," Jackson said. "Hit the EMP again?"

Caleb waited a few seconds before answering. Then: "Alarm's not sounding. Don't know why, and I don't care, but it was our primary reason for the EMP."

"Find him then," Jackson said. "And hurry up about it."

No more words spoken.

Jackson went outside.

Caleb headed up the main staircase.

60

Ogilvy was in full-on panic mode in the master bedroom as he paced about, rambling.

Tatiana was on the floor, hugging her knees against the wall, crying.

Price's face was dead, his lust for vengeance over losing Decker rivaling Jackson's after losing Harper.

"All our men are down," Ogilvy said. "Fucking *Decker* is down. You need to get me the hell out of here."

For the umpteenth time tonight, Price checked his weaponry. Then: "Not yet."

"Not yet? What the fuck do you mean, *'not yet'*? No *way* someone didn't hear that grenade go off. Police are definitely on the way."

"So make a call," Price said.

"What?"

"Make a call to Tredyffrin Township Police. Tell them who you are. Tell them you're visiting your girlfriend in the 'burbs. That the explosion was fireworks or some shit. Your son is with you and he was setting off M-80s in the woods, I don't know."

"At this time of night? What kind of father would let his kid do such a thing?"

"You *aren't* letting your kid do such a thing. Just tell them."

Ogilvy stopped his pacing. Considered it.

Always careful in granting his employer respect, Price was officially out of fucks to give. Only one thing mattered now: Caleb's head on his wall. "Just fucking do it," he said to Ogilvy.

And much like Price was careful to grant Ogilvy respect, yet had run out of fucks to give, so too was Ogilvy's fuck tank empty; he took no issue with Price's harsh order, self-preservation—in stark contrast to Price's vengeance—his motive for that tank being empty.

"Fine," Ogilvy said. Phone already in hand, he started to dial. Paused mid-dial and looked at Price's departing back. "*Where are you going?*"

61

Caleb stood on the landing of the main staircase, SIG SG 550 high and ready. The upstairs, though not as vast as the downstairs, was still considerable. So many rooms. So many closed doors.

Caleb felt that if Ogilvy was anywhere, it would be the master bedroom. Question was, did he have more protection in there? Sure he did. No elite security would leave him to fend for himself, no matter how many bodies they might have heard him and Jackson dispatching downstairs, no matter how sobering the frag in the woods might have been.

But then again, maybe not. If Caleb were in the shoes of that security, he would expect the enemy to make a quick beeline for that master bedroom, and he would therefore choose a neighboring room to occupy, pop out and catch the enemy unaware while they were fixated on hurrying towards the obvious destination.

If they thought like Caleb.

But like Caleb had explained to Parsons about his belief that he was still alive because he refused to believe what assholes had to say, so too did he believe that he was still alive because he never underestimated an assailant; assumed that they thought, and would do, exactly as he might. A bit arrogant maybe, but hell, he was still alive, wasn't he?

And so Caleb crept a few inches at a time. Stopped and listened. Crept a bit more. Stopped and listened.

So far nothing.

Crept. Stopped. Listened.

This time he heard something. A muffled conversation in the distance. But *was* it a conversation? He could only hear one voice doing the talking. A male voice. Someone on the phone? The voice seemed oddly composed. No sense of panic. No shouting.

Caleb crept closer towards the voice in the distance. He passed several doors along the way. Some open, some closed. He paused by each one, adrenaline pulsing, fueling him, ready for someone to pounce from one of those doors.

So far, no one did.

He rounded a corner, spotted two double doors roughly twenty feet ahead. Up until now he had only spotted single doors. The double doors ahead almost certainly led to the master bedroom. The voice was growing in volume too, but it was still just the one. Someone on the phone for sure. Ogilvy? If so, why so composed? The guy should be in a frenzy by now, shouldn't he? Why—*wait*. Was that...was that laughter? Did he just hear *laughter*? None of this made any sense, dammit.

62

There were only two single doors left between Caleb and the double doors ahead, the brief laughter (???) ahead. The one to his right was open. The one to his left closed. The one to his right was a guest bathroom.

Go into the bathroom and flush the toilet? Chances were decent someone might hear it. They might emerge to inspect. He could be waiting with many bullets.

No. If someone was crafty—and Ogilvy's protection was; they thought like him, after all—they would not rush into the bathroom willy-nilly. They would likely creep as he had been doing. Park themselves right outside that bathroom door, wait, listen, take a quick peek, spot him, *boom*—firefight.

And the advantage would *not* be his in such a firefight. Caleb's assailant would have the entire hallway for cover and mobility at their disposal. Caleb would have, well, Caleb would have the guest bathroom, its linear structure giving the assailant a direct line of sight. The assailant could literally poke their gun hand through the doorway while taking cover behind the wall. Fire away until they heard a body drop.

He supposed he could hide behind the shower curtain—he spotted a small shower with said curtain opposite the sink and mirror—and pay homage to *Psycho* with one hell of a surprise when the curtain was drawn.

But that was no good either. His silhouette would be visible through the curtain. Whoever came to investigate would start right on shooting *through* that curtain before he could draw it back. He knew *he* would.

Scratch the bathroom idea.

The double doors ahead were the only viable option. But how to play it?

Charge forward, kick the doors in and start blasting?

Let's run down the hill and fuck one of those cows.

No—let's walk *down and fuck them all.*

He and Jackson had no choice but to run down that hill by hitting the EMP when the keys to the patio doors didn't work. When Ogilvy was pressing him via text about the name of his wife and time was a critical issue.

Time was an issue now too, with the police's impending arrival. But so far, he'd yet to hear anything from Jackson.

Then get your ass in gear before you do.

Fine—but I'm not running down the hill. I'm walking. Fucking walking.

And so Caleb would not run. He would walk. Walk down the hill and fuck them all…if someone wasn't suddenly behind him with a blade to his throat.

63

"Hello, Caleb," a male voice said behind him. The voice removed Caleb's headset and tossed it. Pressed the blade of the knife harder into his throat. "You mind tossing that rifle for me too?"

Why didn't he just shoot me?

He decided to ask. "Why didn't you just shoot me?"

"Because this is more than a little personal to me," the voice said. "A bullet would be too *im*personal. I want your flesh. The man you killed tonight was a brother to me; he would want your flesh too. I plan to give it to him."

The guy's running on emotion. Could be a good thing. Emotion can make you careless. Prime example being his willingness to forgo a bullet in favor of a blade.

"You'll have to be more specific," Caleb said, still facing the double doors, the voice behind him still pressing the blade hard against his throat. "I killed a lot of people tonight."

"The grenade in the woods by your sniper buddy," the voice said.

You wanna give my flesh to that *guy? Good luck finding him.*

"I'm flattered you think I managed such a thing, but I'm afraid all credit goes to my 'sniper buddy' on that one. So, technically, I *didn't* kill him."

The voice pressed the blade deeper into Caleb's throat. Caleb felt the thin sting of the blade and knew it had cut him. "He's dead *because* of you," the voice said.

"Actually, he's dead because of Mr. Ogilvy in there—" Caleb pointed a careful finger towards the double doors with his non-gun hand. "It was your boss that started this mess, not me. So, how about we both go into that master bedroom, ice him together, and call it even."

"Not a chance," the voice said. "And you haven't tossed your rifle yet. Do it now or I'll cut off your cock and choke you with it."

"Yeesh—that's something even *I've* never done. You're pretty hardcore, aren't you, mister...?"

"Price. And you've got three seconds."

Lower the rifle, act like you're about to toss it, and then shoot him in the foot? No. You'd have to look down and back to get a good fix on his foot.

Lower it, pretend you're about to toss it, then just start blasting whatever you can behind you? No again. Rifle's too long; he's pressed up against me. Not enough wiggle room.

Caleb tossed his SIG SG 550. The rifle hit the rug with a muted thud.

"Now hold very still," Price said. "I don't want this to have to end quickly."

"Might not have a choice, Mr. Price. I'd bet my aforementioned cock that police are on their way after that frag outside went off. The real police, I mean. Not the corrupt dickheads you work for."

Price started to pull Caleb's Glock from its holster. "The police won't be showing," he began. "Mr. Ogilvy is on the phone with them now, explaining this evening's commotion." Price tossed

Caleb's Glock. "Mr. Ogilvy is well-known in his department in Philadelphia. He should have no trouble convincing a suburban department to let it go."

Composed voice on the phone explained. Laughter explained.

Price pulled Caleb's tactical knife next. Tossed it. "No one is coming to help you." Price removed Caleb's pack bag and tossed that. "So, it looks like we have all the time in the world."

Caleb felt relief upon hearing this news. True, the news came from a highly-trained security specialist holding a knife to his throat, but Caleb felt it all the same. He did not want the police to show and thwart his plans. He wanted Ogilvy all to himself. The breathing obstacle behind him was all that stood in his way.

Price patted down the rest of Caleb's body to make sure there were no more surprises. There weren't.

Caleb was now armed with only his hands and feet (and head; Caleb loved headbutts, and he was not above biting. In fact, not too long ago, his mother had told Caleb—after one glass of wine too many—that his late father had bitten the nose off of one of the two serial killers that had attacked his family in western Pennsylvania when Caleb was only four. How Caleb hoped he would get the chance to do the same tonight. Make his father proud).

"We good now?" Caleb asked Price.

"*I* am, yes," Price said. "Turn slowly and look at me."

Caleb did. Price had a shaved head and dark eyes. He was a few inches shorter than Caleb's six two. Solidly built like Caleb.

Caleb had expected the all-too-familiar face of vengeance on Price, incapable of any affect other than hate.

Price did not have such a face. He was actually smiling.

And Caleb understood that smile. Empathy was often associated with a *kind* sense of understanding towards one's feelings. Few realized that true empathy was the ability to adopt the mindset of both the good *and* the bad in people. Especially for those who were primarily exposed to the bad throughout their lifetime. Especially for those who may share those same bad impulses. Like Caleb.

Empathy. It was the one thing Caleb clung to when he doubted his psychological makeup. Psychopaths can have empathy, and can, in fact, be quite good at reading and understanding other's emotions. But it was purely on a surface level, the way one might read a book. There was no *emotional* empathy attached to what they read. Cognitive empathy and emotional empathy were night and day.

Caleb was equipped with both. And it was this knowledge that was his lifeline whenever he

(frequently)

questioned his status as a psychopath.

"Enjoying this?" Caleb asked.

"I will be," Price said. He started to play with his earlobe.

"I don't get a knife?"

"You do not." Price raised the knife, tapped the blade against the tip of Caleb's nose. His smile was the devil's smile.

"Not very sporting of you," Caleb said. "Haven't you ever heard of pulthatchery?"

It was a nonexistent word in a question that served no other purpose than to engage Price's brain for a few seconds. It was a trick Caleb had used before. When the brain is engaged with a question, especially a nonsensical one like the one Caleb had just asked, it momentarily hits the pause button, giving the questioner time to act without concern for *reaction*.

Act on something like, oh, disarming a man with a knife?

64

Caleb had learned through experience that wrist locks and other fancy shit commonly taught by "experts" in the field of knife defense were as reliable as politicians.

Caleb's method was simple: clear the weapon, and then blast the fucker as hard and as often as possible.

And so while Price was figuring out just what the hell "pulthatchery" meant, Caleb did just that, knocking the blade away with his left hand, and then driving the heel of his palm under Price's chin with his right.

The blow took Price off his feet, knife coming free and falling to the floor. Caleb had made solid contact with Price's jaw and prayed the man would be snoozing before he hit the deck, but the tough fucker was not; he was recuperating on his back, and quickly.

Caleb bent for the discarded knife. Price spotted Caleb's intentions and went for the pistol holstered on his waist.

Caleb aborted his plan for the knife and dove, landing on top of Price just as he drew the pistol, latched on to his wrist and banged the gun hand repeatedly against the floor.

Price's grip on the pistol was strong; it was not coming free.

Still with an iron grip on Price's wrist, Caleb began slamming headbutts into the asshole's face. When he heard and felt Price's nose crack beneath his forehead, he tried banging Price's gun hand on the floor again.

The pistol finally came free.

Caleb leaned over Price's torso, reaching for the discarded pistol, but Price used his hips to buck Caleb forward, shooting him past the weapon and onto his face.

Price rolled, got to his hands and knees. Whether he was still dazed from the headbutts, or had instead reverted back to his earlier intentions of making this personal with a blade and forgoing the impersonal nature of the gun, Price snatched up the knife instead of the pistol.

Caleb scrambled to his feet, Price rising to his as well, knife in hand, looking unsteady, blood pouring from his shattered nose.

He approached Caleb with caution, no longer smiling.

Caleb backed up. They rounded the corner, Price still creeping forward, wary, Caleb continuing to back away, eyes going all over his surroundings as he did so, looking for something, anything, to level the playing field. Disarming a man with a static blade in your face was one thing, but when the fight was already on? With a knife-wielder who knew how to use it? It was akin to disarming a lawnmower.

And it was pretty much guaranteed that Price knew how to use it. This was *not* the guy who'd been cutting lemons and limes at the bar in Philly. The guy who'd lunged amateurishly at Caleb with a kitchen knife.

Caleb spotted a small wooden end table to his left. The table was displaying a porcelain vase.

Caleb grabbed the vase and threw it at Price. Price evaded, the vase bouncing, not breaking, on the carpeted floor.

Caleb then picked up the end table. Held it by the legs, intent on using its square top as a shield.

Price finally attacked, slashing and stabbing, Caleb successfully defending with the table.

Price changed tactics and went to kick Caleb in the groin. Caleb brought the table's edge down onto Price's rising shin, bone thudding against wood. Price winced, and Caleb thrust the flat of the table into Price like a battering ram. Price saw it coming and lowered his shoulder to mitigate the impact. It worked. Price then lowered his shoulder again and drove it into the table, knocking Caleb back several feet.

They were now at the landing of the main staircase. Caleb looked over his shoulder, spotted the intimidating descent of the staircase. Whipped his head back on Price.

And Price was smiling again, playing with his earlobe again.

Price charged forward like a linebacker, shoulder slamming into the table with terrific force.

Too terrific.

The force drove both Caleb *and* Price (and the table) down the staircase in an anything-but-graceful tumble, Caleb hitting the unforgiving tiled floor first, the table second, clattering away behind Caleb's head, Price third, landing on top of Caleb, the knife in his grasp going the way of the table as it clattered away.

65

Both men were shaken from the fall down the main staircase's considerable stairs. There was a brief moment of pause.

Price collected himself first, rising up on his knees, still atop Caleb and now straddling him in a mount position, and went to drive his fist down into Caleb's face.

Caleb saw it coming and moved his head at the last second, Price's fist hitting the tile with a definitive crack, possibly shattering his hand but without him seeming to notice, adrenaline anesthetizing him to the pain.

Price raised the same fist again, but Caleb bucked him off, Price being pitched face first into the tile just as Caleb had been bucked and pitched face first into the carpet upstairs only moments ago.

Caleb had no time to take pleasure in this fact (his face treated by carpet; Price's with tile), and he quickly found his feet and ran at the still prone Price, keen on punting his head off.

But no, the sturdy bastard had regrouped yet again, got to his hand and knees, saw Caleb's intentions, and rolled away from the kick at the last second.

CALEB: ATONEMENT

Price hopped to his feet. Scanned the floor for the knife. Spotted it, but got no further.

Caleb rushed forward with a flurry of punches, carrying both of them into the kitchen, Price covering up en route, some of the punches getting through, but none of them on the jaw for the KO shot.

One of Caleb's punches caught the elbow of Price's guard, and Caleb felt the knuckles on his ring and pinky finger of his left hand crack and give—the all-too-common boxer's fracture.

But much like adrenaline had anesthetized Price to pain when his fist collided with the tiled floor, so too was Caleb immune to the pain of his broken knuckles. He would still hammer away with that fist, worry about the damage later.

Besides, there was a far more pressing hindrance to be concerned about. Fatigue.

In the movies, two guys could fight for twenty minutes nonstop. In real life, in a real fight, especially when adrenaline was involved, you *maybe* had three minutes before your gas tank was empty, no matter how good your conditioning was.

Caleb was feeling it now. His lungs burned; his limbs felt laden with concrete.

Fortunately, now that Price had momentarily backed off after covering up from Caleb's blitz of punches, Caleb was able to take pleasure (though it was more like relief than pleasure) in the fact that Price too appeared winded—chest heaving, broken nose forcing him to breathe heavily through a mouth that was now framed red from the leak, blood dripping off his chin.

"Don't suppose you want to take me up on my earlier proposal?" Caleb said between pants. "Go upstairs, take out Ogilvy, and then call it even?"

"Fuck your mother," Price said between pants of his own.

Caleb's rage flickered like a red fluorescent light coming to life. Mention of his family always found the switch. This was bad news for anyone, especially now. That rage would provide Caleb with another adrenaline dump, another surge of energy.

He stared hard at Price. And Price, oblivious to the advantage he'd granted Caleb with his insult, only noted that flickering rage in Caleb, mistakenly thinking it wise to take it a step further.

"Ogilvy mentioned your dog. Rosco, is it?" Price said. "He mentioned how upset you'd gotten when Alexander threatened him at your apartment. Mentioned what great leverage your dog's life would make if you got out of line."

The red fluorescent light no longer flickered. It was now alive and well, capable of blinding anyone who was stupid enough to—

"After I'm done with you tonight," Price began, "I'm going to find Rosco, skin him alive, and then bathe him in salt water. How's that sound, Caleb?"

The red fluorescent light exploded from the final surge of power it had been fed.

Caleb's gas tank was full again.

66

Caleb sprinted forward and blitzed Price with more punches. He threw them as fast and as hard as he'd ever done on any human before, Price's guard lacking the protection it previously had as Caleb's heavy fists mashed Price's forearms and hands into his face, rocking him almost as efficiently as an unprotected shot.

Caleb then aborted punches and adopted elbows, latching onto the back of Price's neck and firing them into the man's face, the elbows too mashing Price's crumbling guard until it fell away entirely, Caleb then slamming home a final horizontal elbow into Price's unprotected temple.

Price stumbled back and dropped to a knee. Caleb spotted a utensil drawer. Grabbed its handle and ripped it, not open, but clean out, utensils clanging onto the kitchen floor. He brought the drawer down onto Price's head, the wood cracking on impact. Brought it down a second time, the wood giving this time, the bottom of the drawer splitting in half.

Price fell onto his back. Caleb looked around the enormous kitchen. Spotted a blender on the counter. Went towards it.

Price, heavily stunned, slapped blindly towards the piles of discarded utensils on the kitchen floor. His blind hand found a knife.

Caleb grabbed the blender's heavy glass pitcher by its handle, removed it from its motor base, and approached Price.

Price sat up and plunged the knife deep into Caleb's thigh.

Caleb backed up a step, Price letting go of the handle, the knife stuck rigid in Caleb's leg.

Caleb felt nothing. He looked down at his leg, the knife therein, with a wicked sense of amusement, the way a bully might palm the head of a small victim, keeping the victim just outside out of arm's reach as the smaller kid whiffed punches in the bully's direction.

Caleb took his eyes off the knife and looked at Price. This time, it was Caleb who smiled.

Caleb whipped the blender's heavy pitcher into the side of Price's head. The thick glass shattered on impact, and Price fell onto his back again. This time, the tough bastard was out cold.

Caleb, however, was far from finished.

He first pulled the knife from his thigh and tied off the wound with an apron he spotted hanging from a hook by the sink. The apron showcased a picture of The Swedish Chef from *The Muppet Show*. It made Caleb smile again. He loved the Muppets.

Caleb then picked up the plastic bottom of the pitcher that held its steel blades (and that plastic bottom with its steel blades was all that was left; the pitcher's glass was everywhere), went back to the blender's motor base, and reattached the plastic bottom.

Caleb returned to Price, bent, slapped him in the face a few times until he stirred, grabbed him by the scalp, and then jerked him to his feet with a strength that even impressed Caleb.

Still clutching Price's scalp, Price moaning as he vacillated between consciousness and unconsciousness, Caleb turned the knob on the blender's motor base to the liquefy setting, and hit the power.

The steel blades were a whirring blur on the blender's top speed, the sound just enough to fully wake Price from his stupor.

The last thing Price saw was that whirring blur.

67

Finished, Price's face no longer resembled a face, but something you might find discarded in the back room of a butcher's shop.

Caleb, still holding Price by the scalp, flung him away like the chewed meat he was. The ever-familiar cocktail of righteousness and delight teased his nerve endings, eventually finding their way to his groin. The ever-familiar feeling he both loathed and loved. The ever-familiar feeling that had him constantly questioning his status as a psychopath, despite all previous self-assurances that he, unlike true psychopaths, was equipped with emotional empathy.

And wasn't the second burst of adrenaline that refilled his gas tank all due to love for his family and Rosco? Could a psychopath ever feel such genuine love? He didn't know.

Were love and emotional empathy two different things? They needn't be mutually exclusive, need they? Surely there was some overlap, dammit.

The tingle in his groin was still present. He even had a semi-erection. Before, he would have made a beeline for Dr. Flynn's for release, all kinds of justification for the visit along the way.

Now, Dr. Flynn had insisted on weaning. For him to transition to self-gratification. And after an initial fuss and, later, introspection, he had decided he *wanted* to adhere to Dr. Flynn's proposed method of weaning. That he no longer wanted to feel weak, a slave to his demons.

Right about now would be the ideal time to test such a thing. The self-gratification thing. But Caleb didn't want that either. Perhaps it was Price's recent words about his mother and Rosco that deemed it horribly inappropriate. Or perhaps it was the fact that he was in a stranger's home and that Ogilvy was still upstairs, for fuck's sake. Whipping his dick out now hardly seemed top of the list of priorities.

Or was there something else? Perhaps his desire not to be a slave to his demons was stronger than he thought. Perhaps weaning, much as he respected Dr. Flynn, was unnecessary. Perhaps cold turkey was the way. He was strong enough, dammit.

So Caleb slapped his groin. Actually slapped his own groin, and hard too. It was classic conditioning, the way someone in an unconventional facility might receive an electric shock whenever reaching for a cigarette. They would get a shock whenever they had the urge to smoke, and Caleb would slap his groin whenever he had the urge to, well, whenever he had *the* urge.

And oddly enough, it had worked for now. His semi-erection was gone, as was the urge. Perhaps it had more to do with the need to hurry, to get upstairs to Ogilvy than anything else, but for now he didn't care. It might not have been true cold turkey—more like nicotine gum, he supposed—but again, he didn't care. Baby steps and all.

Then the face on the floor that had once looked like Price made a noise.

Price was still alive.

And try as he might to cling to all the therapy he had just

administered on himself, Caleb could not help but feel the tingle again as an idea came to him.

He knew he should just pluck one of the many scattered knives from the kitchen floor, slash Price's throat, and hurry upstairs to Ogilvy, but Price's earlier threat towards Rosco repeated in his head like a song he wanted nothing more than to forget:

"I'm going to find Rosco, skin him alive, and then bathe him in salt water."

It was just too poetically justified to resist.
Caleb went through the kitchen cupboards,
(*I'm not a psychopath*)
found a large container of Morton Iodized Salt,
(*I'm not a psychopath*)
stuck his fingernail under the little metal tab and opened the spout,
(*I'm* not *a fucking psychopath*)
and poured every last grain of salt over the mangled face that had once looked like Price.

———

Price moaned, a long drawn-out moan like a zombie's wail. And the analogy was accurate in more ways than one—Price's face looked like a zombie's. A particularly ripe one at that.

Other than the moan, Price did nothing else. Likely couldn't. The only thing he *could* manage was to exhale a cloud of salt from the considerable amount that had fallen into his lipless mouth.

Good, choke on it too, fuck face.

Caleb tossed the salt container aside, picked up the sharpest kitchen knife he could find, and promptly slashed Price's throat deep enough to feel the blade scrape his vertebrae beneath.

The tingle was relentless, and Caleb slapped his groin again.

Baby steps, bitches. And I am not *a fucking psychopath.*

He left the kitchen in search of Ogilvy.

68

Caleb did not rush up the main staircase. He took his time, steadying his breath, lowering his heart rate. He was excited to get his hands on Ogilvy, but did not want to fall into the same trap that Price had fallen into—allowing emotion to get the better of good judgment.

Once upstairs, he collected his belongings on the way towards the master bedroom. His headset. His pack bag. His Glock. His knife. His SIG SG 550.

Would Ogilvy be waiting for him in that master bedroom, armed and ready to fire? Maybe. Maybe not. Perhaps he would hesitate, wait for visual confirmation. After all, Caleb could be Price entering that room, carrying with him the good news that Caleb was definitely dead this time.

But would Price just enter? Not if he was smart. Surely someone as seasoned as Price would knock first, confirm his identity in case Ogilvy *was* armed behind those double doors, jumpy and prepared to blast whoever entered.

Knock first. There was an idea.

CALEB: ATONEMENT

And so, standing in front of those double doors now, Caleb did just that. He knocked and waited.

No reply.

He knocked again, tried imitating Price's voice as best as he could remember it. Kept his tone intentionally low the way actors often did while emulating a foreign accent they weren't entirely comfortable with.

"It's Price," Caleb said. "Can I come in?"

"Come in." It was a female's voice. And Caleb needn't be a brain surgeon to deduce that it was Tatiana's voice.

Had Ogilvy told her to respond? Recognized Caleb's try at imitating Price's voice and was thus using her as bait, Tatiana in the center of the room to occupy Caleb's direct line of sight when he entered, Ogilvy pressed tight to the wall next to those double doors, ready to blow his head off the moment he entered?

How to play it?

Caleb attempted a slow turn on one of the crystal doorknobs. It didn't budge. And he was grateful for that. Whoever was in the room had locked the doors for their safety and forgotten they'd locked them. That meant they would have to come to him.

"Door's locked," Caleb said, still keeping his tone low, still trying to sound like Price. *Risk saying more? Fuck it.* "Can you open it for me?"

A pause.

Caleb let go of his rifle and let it hang by its strap, opting instead for his Glock. He wanted one hand free. If Ogilvy opened that door, he would empty his Glock's entire magazine into him before he could draw his last breath. If a woman opened it, he would snatch her with that free hand, pull her out into the hallway with him, and then wait for a sign that Ogilvy was inside—a commotion, an utterance, whatever.

And if he got that sign? He would use that same free hand to draw a flashbang from his pack bag. Roll the stun grenade into the master bedroom, wait for the flash and boom, and then stroll on in and formally introduce himself to Mr. Sam Ogilvy.

Caleb knocked again.

"Hang on a sec," the woman on the other side of the double doors said.

Sounds of a lock clicking.

Caleb readied himself.

The door opened. A beautiful woman greeted him.

Caleb reached out, grabbed the lapel of the red silk robe she was wearing, and pulled her out into the hallway with him.

The woman went to speak, but Caleb immediately placed a hand over her mouth and pressed her up against the wall adjacent to the double doors. Listened intently for signs of Ogilvy in the bedroom.

He didn't hear anything.

Throw the flashbang anyway? He took his hand off the woman's mouth.

"He's—"

"*Shut up!*" Caleb whisper yelled.

Caleb listened some more. Still could not hear any sign of Ogilvy. He pulled the flashbang from his pack bag.

The woman saw the grenade in Caleb's hand. Her eyes bulged. "Oh my God! *He's not here!*"

Caleb spun towards her. Her fear alone was decent enough confirmation of the truth, but decent enough was no good so close to the finish line. Caleb pressed the tip of his Glock's suppressor into her chest.

"*Don't you fucking lie to me!*" he continued to whisper yell. "*I will kill you here and now.*"

The woman instinctively raised both hands, eyes wider than ever. "*I'm not lying! I swear to God!*"

"She's not lying," Jackson said into Caleb's headset. "He did leave."

Caleb blinked several times, a computer on the fritz as it processed too much at once. Then: "He *what?*" he said to Jackson. "You let him fucking—"

"*Eeeasy* there, champ," Jackson said. "Come on outside; I've got a surprise for you."

69

Before Caleb headed outside to meet Jackson and receive his surprise, he holstered his Glock and put the flashbang back into his pack bag.

"You sure that's not going to go off?" the woman asked, looking at Caleb's bag.

"We're good," he said. "You Tatiana?"

"Yeah. How did you know my name?"

"Same way you probably know mine."

"Is it Caleb?"

"It is."

"You're supposed to be like an assassin or something?"

"Or something."

"All the guys Sam brought with him, are they…?"

"You tell me. Any more running around I should know about?"

"Sam said all his men were down. Even Decker. I don't know about Price."

"Decker. Were he and Price close?"

Tatiana nodded. "I never saw them apart."

"Okay—well, Price is dead too then," Caleb said.

Tatiana dropped her head and started to fidget.

"I don't plan on making you join them," Caleb said, "but you never can tell."

Tatiana took a step back.

"If I leave you here, you think you might be making any phone calls?" Caleb asked.

Tatiana shook her head.

"Got a cell phone?"

Tatiana went into the pocket of her robe and produced a phone.

Caleb held out his hand. Tatiana gave it to him without hesitation.

Caleb put the phone in his pack bag. "I'm assuming there's a landline here?" he then asked.

Tatiana nodded.

Caleb bluffed her. "My team will find and track any outgoing calls from that landline. If I find out that you did make a call, then I promise I won't hesitate to make sure you and Ogilvy are canoodling in hell. That clear?"

She nodded again. Then: "What about…" She paused, clearly uncertain how to phrase it. "What about the bodies?"

"Rival drug gang, if you ask me."

Tatiana looked at the floor. "I'm not a bad person," she said.

"Never said you were. But my promise—not threat—still stands."

"He's an asshole," Tatiana said. "I wouldn't risk my life over him."

"Just spread your legs and take money from him."

She lifted her head, contempt on her face.

"No judging," Caleb said. "I can assure you, I've done worse. But I'd suggest looking for a new sugar daddy. Preferably one a bit more on the up and up."

"Are any of them?" she said.

Caleb considered the inherently selfish nature of men, which he believed few truly grew out of.

"No," Caleb eventually said, "I suppose not."

"Still, it beats working," Tatiana said, offering up a pitiful chuckle after.

Men and *women*, Caleb amended. *We fucking deserve each other.*

"Take care, Tatiana…and please remember that I always keep my promises."

70

Once Caleb was outside, Jackson told him that he was back at their cars on the side of the road, one hundred yards east of the house.

Jackson was smoking a cigarette by his vehicle when Caleb arrived.

"Unless my surprise is Ogilvy tied up in your trunk, then I don't fucking want it." And Caleb meant every word. If Jackson had spotted Ogilvy leaving and had done nothing about it, then their adventures were far from done, and such a notion was as appealing as starting the whole evening over again—his second gas tank was bone dry; the knife wound on his thigh throbbed.

"Uncanny," Jackson said, and popped his trunk.

Inside was Ogilvy. His wrists and ankles were bound with plastic zip ties. His mouth was covered with duct tape. His nose was crusted with blood, his right eye swollen.

Caleb's gas tank might have been empty, but his pleasure tank was spilling over. He looked at Jackson. "You'd think I'd have learned not to underestimate you after tonight."

Jackson didn't reply. Perhaps his mind was back on Harper after Caleb's mention of what had transpired tonight.

Caleb's mind went towards Harper as well, but

(*emotional*)

empathy would have to wait to be fully indulged. Caleb bent over the open trunk. "Evening, Sam. We've never been formally introduced."

Ogilvy fought his binds and yelled something into the duct tape.

"I'd wager he's threatening us," Caleb said. "Gotta admire his optimism. You should be taking notes."

Jackson took a final drag of his cigarette and flicked it, orange sparking on the dark road. He exhaled in Caleb's direction.

Caleb waved away the smoke. "I'm going to assume that your decision to stay put and have a smoke means you know the police aren't coming," he said.

"I know," Jackson said.

"How'd you find out?"

Jackson gestured towards Ogilvy's battered face. "Beat it out of him," he said matter-of-factly, as though it should have been obvious.

"Works for me." Caleb turned back to Ogilvy. "Night's still young, Sam. If you saw what I did to your buddy Price, you'd know what a terrifying prospect that is for a guy in your position."

Ogilvy hollered into the duct tape again.

"Yep—sure do have to admire that optimism."

"You just gonna talk to him all night?" Jackson asked.

Caleb pulled his tactical knife. Considered it, then put it away.

Caleb had flashed on one of the few memories he had of his father. How his father would give him a little bit of money, and how Caleb would then ask to head to the nearest candy store so that he could get his immediate sugar fix. His father telling him he would happily take him, but wouldn't it be so much more rewarding to save that money; buy yourself something bigger and better down the road, something that would last longer, something you could enjoy indefinitely.

Such a life lesson might have understandably fallen on deaf ears for a child, and for Caleb it often did; foresight at such an age seldom saw further than that candy store. But now, as an adult, in this precise moment, that foresight was a Hubble Space Telescope.

Caleb went through Ogilvy's pockets, pulled his cell phone, and then stuffed it into his pack bag along with Tatiana's and Alexander's. He then slammed the trunk shut, took out his car keys, and handed them to Jackson.

"Take my car," Caleb said.

Jackson, frowning with curiosity the moment Caleb had sheathed his knife, frowned with even deeper curiosity now. He took the keys all the same.

"Gimme yours," Caleb said.

"Why?"

"Please."

Jackson handed them over.

Caleb opened the driver's side door to Jackson's car. "Follow me," he said.

71

Jackson waited outside of Dylan's Den in Caleb's idling car. In front of him was his car, Ogilvy still very much alive inside the trunk.

Caleb knew the bookstore would be closed. He also knew that Dylan would still be inside, but it was no hunch; he'd called Dylan on the road and told her it would be in her best interest to meet him there.

She was waiting by the shop window. Let Caleb in, and then locked the glass door behind them.

The store was predominantly dark, only a few lamps lit here and there, providing just enough light. Caleb followed Dylan towards the back. He spotted Harper on her east sill—moonbathing?—and blew her a kiss.

In Dylan's humble quarters now. The lights on.

"Is he dead?" Dylan asked.

"No."

Dylan's face was one of immediate panic.

"All his men are, though. Even his elite protection."

"Well, then where is *he*?"

"Outside. In my trunk."

"*What?*"

Caleb ignored her. "Here's what's going to happen now, Dylan: you're going to do what you do best. You're going to gather up every single piece of incriminating evidence you have on Ogilvy, and then you're going to hand it over to me. You do that—and I mean *every. Single. Piece*—and I'm on my way. You'll never see me again, but more importantly, you'll never see Ogilvy again."

Caleb set Tatiana's phone, Alexander's phone, and Ogilvy's phone beside one of Dylan's many laptops on her table, all of the laptops currently closed. "This should help with some of those pieces." Caleb thrummed his fingers on one of the laptop lids. "What do you say, Dylan? Can you do that, you think?"

"I can do that."

"Great. I take my tea with milk and two sugars."

72

**SCI Phoenix - Pennsylvania Department of Corrections
Collegeville, Pennsylvania**

Sam Ogilvy was lying on his cot, reading his newest edition of *Food & Wine Magazine*, when he heard the unmistakable clack, clack of a correctional officer's boots on concrete growing closer.

"Afternoon, Ogilvy," the officer said.

Ogilvy tossed the magazine and sat bolt upright in his cot. He stared hard at the officer through the iron bars. "It's *Miller*," Ogilvy said in hushed tones. *"John Miller.* You know that, you asshole."

The officer made a theatrical *whoops!* face. "Sorry. Afternoon, Miller."

"Don't give me 'sorry,'" Ogilvy said. "I'll talk to the warden and have you cleaning fucking toilets by nightfall."

"Your threats are as hollow as your head, Miller. Soon you'll realize who *really* runs this prison. Especially if you keep calling me an asshole."

Ogilvy didn't appear fazed in the slightest. "What do you want?"

"Got a visitor," the officer said.

"I don't have any scheduled."

"Call it an impromptu visit."

Ogilvy frowned. "What the hell are you talking about?"

Caleb Lambert appeared next to the officer. He was dressed in a pricey suit befitting a top-tier attorney. "Afternoon, *John*."

Ogilvy sprang from his cot and rushed towards the iron bars. He gripped them as though the floor had just dropped out from under him. "*What the hell is this?*" he hissed, any previous anger he held for the officer over the use of his real name paling in comparison to what he now projected the officer's way. "*You are in violation of every conceivable—*"

"John, John…" Caleb interrupted. "Settle down, please."

Now Ogilvy flicked his anger Caleb's way. Still in a dramatic whisper: "*You can stand there as cocky as you like, you little prick, but my lawyer—and he's a* good *fucking lawyer; his hourly rate is probably more than you make in a month—has assured me that it won't be long before you're standing where I am. That I'll be the one on the other side of these bars, looking in at you with that smug fucking face of yours.*"

"Yeah, yeah—we all know how clever your attorney is. Arranging a different identity for you with the warden so the inmates don't learn that you're actually a cop." Caleb raised his voice on "cop."

Ogilvy waved around two frantic hands while shushing Caleb. "*Goddammit, you are violating my fucking rights!*" He looked at the officer again. "Both *of you are!*"

"Here's the thing, though, John," Caleb began, "I actually make quite a bit of money each month. Frank here can attest to that, right, Frank?" Caleb placed his hand on the officer's shoulder.

"Oh, yes," Frank said.

"College tuition these days is brutal," Caleb went on. "And on a corrections officer's salary? I mean, it hardly seems fair, does it, Frank?"

Frank nodded. "It's tough."

"But not anymore, right?" Caleb said. "Your daughter's even going to be getting a semester abroad, yeah? Italy? Already bought and paid for?"

"I've never seen her so happy," Frank said.

"What is this?" Ogilvy said. *"What is this?"*

"Well, like Frank mentioned earlier, it won't be long now until you figure out who truly runs this prison."

"Meaning what? Meaning *what?*"

"Meaning that John Miller doesn't have much time left, I'm afraid. Sam Ogilvy? Corrupt chief of police, likely responsible for putting a good number of these inmates away, some of them unjustly perhaps?" Caleb splayed a hand. *"That* guy has all the time in the world. Well…until the other inmates stop having fun with him, that is."

"No, no, no, no—you can't do this," Ogilvy said.

"It's done, Sam. Tuition's already paid for in full. Frank here is even using the money he's gonna save to take his wife to—" He looked at the officer. "Where you going again, Frank?"

"Turks and Caicos."

Caleb whistled. "I hear it's amazing there. But you won't leave before spreading our little secret, will you, Frank?"

"No chance."

"Beautiful. You take care now, Sam. I'd tell you not to bend over for the soap, but that's a little played out, isn't it?" Caleb looked at Frank for confirmation.

"A little. But it's still pretty darn accurate," Frank said. "Especially when officers look the other way."

"And they *will* be looking the other way, won't they, Frank?"

"Oh yes."

"Spread some green love their way too, didn't I?" Caleb said.

"Generously."

"Money makes the world go 'round, right, Sam? I imagine no one knows that better than you." Caleb offered a tranquil smile. He could have been a man standing in a day spa instead of a prison. "This turned out to be a really good day."

"Please—I'll do anything. *Anything.*"

"What the hell could you possibly do for me, Sam? Price and Decker are dead. Alexander is dead. All your little foot soldiers are dead. *Real* police want you to rot in here. The truth about you is out, Sam. Except in here, of course. But that won't be for much longer—Frank will see to that."

A sudden thought then occurred to Caleb. His eyes sparkled when he looked at Ogilvy and said: "How about a sugar daddy? You know all about sugar daddies, right, Sam? Maybe, just maybe, you can find yourself one in here. His protection can be like the fancy homes and money you gave Tatiana and all the other women you had. And your payment to him can be, well, I guess it would be very similar to how Tatiana and the others repaid *you*, wouldn't it?" Caleb looked at Frank. "What do they call it? Turning someone out? Making him a bitch?"

"Either one works," Frank said.

Caleb's serene smile became a grin. He was now a man at a card table with an unbeatable hand, the pot astronomical.

Ogilvy did not say another word. Just slunk back to his cot, laid down, and curled up into the fetal position, facing the wall.

Caleb patted Frank on the shoulder. They exchanged a smile. They talked about what Frank and his wife were planning to do in Turks and Caicos as Frank walked Caleb out.

73

Caleb called Nick on his way to Dr. Flynn's house.

"You're alive," Nick answered. He sounded happy to hear from him.

"Unless this is someone else with my phone." Caleb was annoyed with himself that he hadn't thought to use a voice changer to fuck with Nick.

"How did it go?" Nick asked.

"You answered your own question a few seconds ago."

"By saying you're alive?"

"Correct."

"I meant, how did *everything* go? Thomas and Faye told me you ended up contacting them for help."

Caleb still felt bad about that. "Yeah," was all he said. "Give them a call and patch me in."

Nick did.

"You're alive," Thomas said.

"You guys are champs at the bleeding obvious."

"Bleeding?" Nick said.

"It's a British expression," Faye said. "Australian too, I think."

"As usual, Faye is the smartest of you lot." *You lot*. Another common British expression. Caleb was fond of the UK's colloquialisms and idioms. Some of his personal favorites being "bell end" for the head of a penis, denoting a stupid or annoying person, and "touching cloth" or the "turtle's head," denoting one being close to shitting themselves.

"How did everything turn out?" Faye asked. "Was the information Thomas and I gave you helpful?"

"Very. I'm officially in the clear. Those who needed killing are dead, and the one who really needed killing is in prison, though I imagine he's probably dead by now too. Either that or he's currently ironing his new beau's underwear."

Caleb heard Thomas snort.

"Any injuries?" Nick asked.

"I'm good." Caleb thought of Harper. Thought about mentioning it, but didn't.

"Thank God," Faye said.

"Yeah. Listen, vacation time is officially over. Back to work tomorrow."

All three voiced their consent.

"Where are you now?" Faye asked.

"On my way to pick up Rosco. See you in the morning."

"We're glad you're okay," Faye said.

"Stop," Caleb said.

"Stop what?" Faye said.

"Stop being glad I'm okay. One day I won't be. Get used to that idea now. And don't you ever let emotion get in the way of your better judgment. I don't pay you to be my friends. Are we clear?"

A pause and then: "Clear," Faye said.

"Clear," Nick and Thomas said simultaneously.

"See you in the morning."

Caleb hung up. He often cursed his filter, or lack thereof, but he did not regret a word of what he'd just said. Much as he did care for his team, what he'd said needed saying; they needed reminding.

Unnecessary attachments made you vulnerable. Caleb was still alive because he refused to believe what assholes had to say; he never underestimated an assailant; and he never formed unnecessary attachments.

Yet in only a few hours' time, Caleb would prove himself a hypocrite after talking to Parsons.

74

Dr. Flynn was her usual stoic self when Caleb picked up Rosco. A "hello" and "goodbye" was practically all Caleb got.

She did not ask about where he had been, or whether he was all right. Caleb had started to tell her how he was moving into a better head space in regards to their arrangement, her weaning of his needs, but she merely told him to save it for their next session in that stoic way of hers. And had Rosco not been chirping and whining at his side, desperately trying to climb his leg, Caleb might have been a little bothered by it.

But of course Rosco *was* chirping and whining at his side, desperately trying to climb his leg, and any bother Caleb might have felt for Dr. Flynn's response had left just as quickly as it had arrived.

Caleb remembered how, back in Tatiana's home, Jackson had obliterated a foot soldier after learning of Harper's death. How Jackson's pained face had returned to its stony self, moments later, Caleb then confirming, and not for the first time, that vengeance beat Prozac any day of the week.

He was wrong.

Rosco beat Prozac any day of the week. Hell, in Caleb's world, Big Pharma itself was Rosco's bitch.

75

Parsons picked up on the third ring. Another FaceTime. Parsons was sporting a thin moustache.

"Who you going for this time?" Caleb asked.

"Eddie Murphy?"

"Well, he's not as handsome as Denzel or Idris Elba, in my opinion, so I guess that's a start. Unfortunately, Eddie Murphy is one of the greatest comedians of all time."

"You saying I'm not funny?"

"I wouldn't quit your day job."

Parsons looked away.

"And there it is again," Caleb said. "I told you this was going to be a to-be-continued chat, and here we are. What the hell is going on with you, man?"

"You heard from Jackson?" Parsons asked.

Caleb knew Parsons was deflecting, but the subject of Harper's death was too raw to call him on it just yet.

"I haven't since we parted ways in Philadelphia, no," Caleb said. "You?"

"Just once," Parsons said.

"How's he doing?"

"Been drinking his breakfast, lunch, and dinner."

"Ah shit." Caleb hesitated a moment, unsure how to phrase what he wanted to say next. "Does he...does he blame me?"

"Not at all," Parsons said. "He knew what he was getting into."

"And you? You blame me?"

"You *are* to blame, Caleb. But much like I made my own choice to help you in Noodle, costing the lives of good people, so too did Jackson make a choice. You might have been the catalyst—doing what it is that you do—but you never forced us to take part. Free will is a double-edged sword."

This was true. And while the guilt was already strong before Caleb had even started the FaceTime, hearing Parsons voice it as straightforward as he did made it that much stronger.

Now it was Caleb who looked away.

"What's done is done," Parsons said. "Jackson will be okay. Can't promise he'll join you on your next adventure, but he'll be okay."

Caleb looked at Parsons again and nodded.

No more deflecting. "Tell me what's going on in Noodle," Caleb said. "Why have you been avoiding the subject when something is clearly wrong?"

Parsons sighed. "You remember that quaint little town out in the middle of nowhere? The one where people didn't lock their doors at night, and everybody knew everybody?"

"Of course I do."

"It's become a shithole. Something out of the Wild West—gun fights, corruption, gangs, you name it."

Caleb remembered all too well how he'd first likened Noodle to a town straight out of the Old West. *Sans* violence, that is.

Now, according to Parsons, that likeness was as apt as ever, *avec* violence—the missing piece to truly bring the analogy together.

"Ah shit." Caleb sighed. "How many deputies you have getting your back?"

"Two."

"*Two?*"

"Brought on six, initially, but three of them quit."

Caleb frowned. "So you've got three, not two"—Caleb immediately caught himself—"ohhh…"

"Yeah. The three that quit did so shortly after Colin was killed."

"Jesus, man…"

"Yeah," Parsons said again.

"You gotta bring in more help then, Chip. Not deputies, but something heavier. Make some calls to your connections in Indianapolis."

"Can't do it."

"Why?"

"Things are…things are complicated right now."

"Complicated how? Don't lie to me, Chip, and don't play it off like it's nothing."

"Let's just say my family is involved."

"Family? I thought your wife passed—"

"My son."

"You never mentioned you had a son."

Parsons just shrugged.

"Okay, fine—you have a son. How does he factor into all of this?"

"Like I said, it's complicated."

Caleb stood and headed into his bedroom. Pulled a duffel bag from his closet and tossed it onto his bed. Started opening dresser drawers, pulling out clothes, and tossing them on top of the duffel bag. He did it all with one hand; the phone was in the other.

"What are you doing?" Parsons said. He could see everything. "Caleb, what are you doing?"

"I'm good with complicated things," Caleb said, continuing to pack.

"No. Caleb, *no*."

"Too late—already out the door."

"*Caleb!—*"

Caleb hung up and turned off his phone for now.

Rosco jumped up on the bed, looked at the duffel bag, crawled on top of it, lay down, and then looked up at Caleb with those soulful black eyes of his. He knew. Of course he knew. Didn't all pets, the psychic buggers? And oh how contrasting their behavior could be with that psychic ability. Trip to the vet? Nowhere to be found. But going out of town? Not if I'm on your suitcase you can't...unless you take me with you.

Could he? *Should* he? No way would Dr. Flynn agree to take him again. Kennel was, as always, out of the question. Thomas and Faye? Nick?

Rosco barked. *Yes, you should take me with you*, the psychic bugger's bark said.

Caleb considered it. This was not like the last two times. No trained assassins gunning for him. No crooked cops hiding in plain sight as wiseguys with elite security watching their back. He was just visiting an old friend to see whether he could help him out somehow. Help him out with whatever the hell was going on with his son.

Never form any unnecessary attachments.

But Noodle turning into a shithole was his fault, was it not? Didn't he have a responsibility to try to, ahem, wipe it?

Parsons's words coming back to him: *"...you never forced us to take part. Free will is a double-edged sword."*

"Then I'm exercising *my* free will," he said to himself. "And a double-edged sword can be deadly in the right hands."

Deadly to whom?

"Those dumb enough to get in my way."

The innocent people that died in Noodle—were they in your way?

"No, they weren't. I fucked up. And that's why I'm exercising my free will now to go and make it right."

You exercised free will in that Applebee's and look at the mess you got yourself into. In your wildest dreams did you ever think it would escalate as it did? Face it; you have no way of knowing what free will can bring.

"No one does. Nothing is predetermined. Our lives aren't mapped out for us like some paint-by-numbers bullshit."

This is about guilt, isn't it? Guilt for what happened in Noodle. For what happened to Harper. You've been absolved of it all. Why risk making it worse?

"I won't."

Said every guy or girl ever who went in with good intentions, which, as we all know, are never enough.

"I've got more than good intentions. I've got the skills to back it up."

And yet those people in Noodle are still dead. Why not just stay and do your job? Continue to punish bad people?

"I *will* be punishing bad people. Better yet, I'll be saving good people from getting hurt, not punishing the bad *after* the fact."

I think this is an ego thing. A selfish thing. Jackson and Parsons have forgiven you, but that's not enough, is it? You need to prove something to yourself. Dare I mention pride before the fall?

"I won't fall."

Wanna know the surest way not to drown? One that does *involve free will?*

"What?"

Choose not to get into the fucking water.

"Why stop there? How about never driving a car lest someone plow into you? Never leaving the house lest a deranged gunman shoot up the place you happened to be visiting that day? Never getting out of fucking bed lest you fall down the stairs and break your neck on the way to make breakfast? I won't live in fear. Been to that party, thank you. Now *I'm* the one who brings the fear as I choose. The. Fucking. End."

If only.

Caleb sighed and looked out his bedroom window. A praying mantis clung to the outside of the screen behind the windowpane. Caleb approached it.

He had once read that a praying mantis was considered good luck in certain cultures and religions. Some Native Americans believed the insect came before the creation of man and Earth, that the bug represents large families and the cycle of life.

Some Christians believed that the praying mantis represents spiritualism or piety and, if found in your home, may mean that angels were watching over you.

Caleb was not a religious man, but today he would be going with the Christians. Angels watching over him sounded just fine, thanks. Besides, the last thing he wanted was a large family.

He was going. He was going to help the town. Help the people. Help his friend.

Help yourself. So much for never forming any unnecessary attachments, you fucking hypocrite. That rule has served you well thus far. Let's hope exercising your free will to blatantly oppose it pans out, "lest" you're back here in due time with even more regret.

"Fuck off."

Rosco barked again.

Caleb turned away from the praying mantis and looked at his dog. Again, that psychic ability on the little bugger—it was as though he'd read every opposing thought Caleb hadn't voiced.

"What's up, brother?" he asked Rosco.

Rosco barked and started wagging his tail again: *Take me, take me, take me...*

Your dog in the room is now the elephant in the room, isn't he?

Caleb glanced back at the praying mantis. He stared at it without seeing it, his mind elsewhere. Try as his ego did to shut his conscience down, Caleb now realized that at least one of his arguments was false.

He *did* live in fear.

Fear of losing Rosco. Fear of losing his family. Fear of losing his team.

But was that such a bad thing? Didn't we all truly live in fear over the thought of losing a loved one?

Only a psychopath would feel otherwise.

And that was definitely a good thing.

Because he wasn't a psychopath. No self-assuring mantra this time either. He was *not*.

He loved his dog. He loved his family. Even loved his team (though he'd never tell them that).

And while the universe could be arbitrary in who it chose to leave its realm, there were actions one could take in order to mitigate that arbitrariness. None of those actions were foolproof, of course—the universe's sense of humor being as sick as it was—but they sure as hell helped stack the odds in one's favor.

Never picking up a cigarette in order to try to avoid cancer.

Eating right, keeping trim, and exercising in order to try to avoid diabetes, stroke, or heart attack.

Leaving your dog safely behind while you're in Noodle in order to try to avoid—?

"Yes."

Are we actually agreeing on something?

Caleb turned back to Rosco. They stared at one another. Rosco's tail had stopped wagging. He didn't bark, didn't chirp, didn't even whine. It had become a bizarre staring contest between man and canine.

I can leave him with Thomas and Faye.

Rosco broke eye contact, jumped off the duffel bag, and left the room.

Psychic bugger.

Caleb finished packing for Noodle.

AUTHOR'S NOTE

Thank you so much for reading *Caleb: Atonement*, my friends. Looks like Caleb managed to survive yet another colossal mess, but will he be so lucky when he returns to Noodle? And speaking of Noodle: just what the *hell* is going on there now, and why does Parsons want him to stay away? So many questions…

Please know that every single reader is important to me. Whenever I'm asked what my writing goals are, my number one answer, without pause, is to entertain. I want you to have fun reading what I write. I want to make your heart race. I want you to get paper cuts (or Kindle thumb?) from turning the pages so fast. Again—I want to entertain you.

If I succeeded in doing that, I would be very grateful if you took a few minutes to write a review on Amazon for *Caleb: Atonement*. Good reviews can be very helpful, and I absolutely love to read the various insights from satisfied readers.

Thank you so very much, my friends. Until next time…

Jeff Menapace

ABOUT THE AUTHOR

A native of the Philadelphia area, Jeff Menapace has published multiple works in both fiction and non-fiction. In 2011 he was the recipient of the Red Adept Reviews Indie Award for Horror.

Jeff's terrifying debut novel *Bad Games* became a #1 Kindle bestseller that spawned four acclaimed sequels. The series has recently been optioned for feature film and is currently being translated for multiple foreign audiences.

His other novels, along with his award-winning short works, have also received international acclaim and are eagerly waiting to give you plenty of sleepless nights.

Free time for Jeff is spent watching horror movies, The Three Stooges, and mixed martial arts. He loves steak and more steak, thinks the original 1974 *Texas Chainsaw Massacre* is the greatest movie ever, wants to pet a lion someday, and hates spiders.

He currently lives in Pennsylvania with his wife Kelly and their cats Sammy, Bear, and Baby Girl.

Jeff loves to hear from his readers. Please feel free to contact him to discuss anything and everything, and be sure to visit his website to sign up for his FREE newsletter (no spam, not ever) where you will receive updates and sneak peeks on all future works along with the occasional free goodie!

Connect with Jeff on Facebook, Twitter, LinkedIn, Goodreads, and Instagram. Follow Jeff on BookBub and Amazon to get the latest alerts on new releases!

facebook.com/JeffMenapace.writer
twitter.com/JeffMenapace
instagram.com/jeffmenapace
linkedin.com/in/jeffmenapace
bookbub.com/authors/jeff-menapace
goodreads.com/jeffmenapace
amazon.com/-/e/B004R09M0S

ALSO BY JEFF MENAPACE

Please visit Jeff's Amazon Author Page or his website for a complete list of all available works!

https://www.amazon.com/-/e/B004R09M0S

www.jeffmenapace.com

Printed in Great Britain
by Amazon